LAUREN WRIGHT DOUGLAS

NINTH LIFE

NAIAD

1994

Printed in the United States of America on acid-free paper
First Edition
Second printing, August 1994

Edited by Christine Cassidy
Cover design by Catherine Hopkins
Typeset by Sandi Stancil

Library of Congress Cataloging-in-Publication Data

Douglas, Lauren Wright, 1947–
   Ninth life / by Lauren Wright Douglas.
      p.   cm.
   ISBN 0-941483-50-9
   I. Title.
PS3554.08263N5   1989
813'.54—dc20

                                    89-34012
                                        CIP

For all the Jeoffreys

Books by Lauren Wright Douglas

SUNDAY

Chapter 1

Midnight.

I sank a little lower in the front seat of my MG and sipped the last of my Scotch-laced coffee. Parked here in the shadows of Murphy's Auto Repairs, the MG lined up with half a dozen wounded road warriors, I was all but invisible. And bored. I had nothing to do but listen to the creak of Murphy's rickety sign as it swayed in the wind, and watch the occasional pair of car headlights go past on the road to the airport. And wait. I am not a patient waiter.

A particularly icy gust of wind swept across the

highway from the ocean, and I shivered, zipping my windbreaker higher and jamming my hands into my pockets. Why hadn't I remembered my gloves? Late October on Vancouver Island is definitely gloves weather. I wiggled my fingers, and the note I had received — the note which had brought me to this desolate stretch of highway — crinkled in my palm. It had come to my home by registered mail two days ago. Written in longhand on a page torn from a yellow lined writing tablet, it read:

I need to hire you to take delivery of a package. Please meet me at the Donut Stop on Saanich Highway at midnight on Sunday, October 25. Thanks.

Shrew

High melodrama indeed! But the note had come accompanied by ten crisp one-hundred-dollar bills, which were now reposing safely in my wallet. If, as the wags say, money talks, then those ten crisp bills positively warbled. For I was broke. I might ordinarily have turned down such a strange proposition, but October had been a rough month. In the course of two weeks, I had to treat myself to a root canal and a rebuilt engine for my MG. Ouch. My savings account was dead empty. So I made an exception to my own First Commandment (Thou Shalt Take No Off-the-Wall Clients) and agreed to this nocturnal rendezvous. However, just to be on the safe side, I parked one establishment down from the Donut Stop, at Murphy's. This situation was tailor-made for a set-up, and I had no intention of being the settee. I'd let Shrew drive up to the Donut Stop and then decide if I wanted to take this mysterious package.

"Okay, Shrew," I muttered. "It's midnight. I'm freezing my hindquarters off and missing my sleep. Let's get on with it."

But nothing happened. The wind moaned a little louder through the branches of the Garry oaks, Murphy's sign creaked more ominously, and a tangle of paper cups, hamburger wrappers, and newspapers went scudding across the deserted parking lot in a crazy polka. Somewhere nearby an owl hooted — a mournful, tremulous sound. I turned, checking out the parking lot for gremlins, and saw the bulk of Mount Douglas looming like a mute, hulking beast against the sky. Suddenly I remembered — in a few days it would be Hallowe'en, the night when witches were abroad, speeding along the roads on their errands of mischief. I snorted. In North America, Hallowe'en has become nothing more than a children's celebration, a meaningless night of freeloading and silly costumes. But Hallowe'en is a Celtic celebration, and in my family, anyhow, Hallowe'en was a very special day. It marked the end of autumn and the beginning of winter, and on the Rhys farm in Wales, huge bonfires called *Samhnagen* had been lighted year after year for centuries to call the poor shivering ghosts of our family's dead in from their wanderings.

Although I had certainly never seen such a bonfire, the idea was oddly appealing. My grandmother Meadhbh (or, in the anglicized version she hated — Maeve) explained it all to me when I was very young. If farmers took pains to move cows and sheep from the summer pastures into the barns where they could be cared for during the winter, should they do any less for the spirits of their beloved departed? No, she stated firmly. Farmers always lit bonfires on the hills to call the newly dead home for one evening of warmth and hospitality before they went on their way to the spirit world. I know Meadhbh was disappointed that we couldn't have a *Samhnagen* in the little bungalow where we lived in Ottawa, but life in the modern world was a constant disappointment to her.

As was I, I reflected. The night she died, she took my hands in hers and made me promise to build her a *Samhnagen*. Faithless grandchild that I was, I never had.

While I brooded, watching the night sky, a silver fingernail paring of moon pushed its way out from behind Mount Doug and hung in the sky like a crack in the curtained window of heaven. I was getting morose, thinking of my Grandma and my childhood, and resolved to put such thoughts aside. Where the hell was Shrew, anyhow? I peeled back my sleeve and looked at my watch. Twenty after twelve. Ten more minutes, then I was heading home to a hot bath and my bed.

A pair of headlights turned into the little Donut Stop parking lot, and I sat up straight. At last. With a protesting squeal of tires, a dark-colored VW Bug roared into the lot and stopped, motor idling.

I slipped out the driver's door of the MG, keeping the bulk of Murphy's clients between me and the VW, and crept through the shadows until I was behind Shrew's car. A battered Honda Civic and ten feet of asphalt were now all that lay between us. Finally the

6

VW's driver rolled down the window and a curly, blonde head emerged. The driver was clearly taking a good look around.

As was I. If this was a setup, it was too clever for me. I had checked things out pretty thoroughly earlier, and was as sure as I could be that there wasn't another soul anywhere. Still, I patted the bulk of my .357 as I straightened up from the shadows and walked up to the driver's side of the VW, nice and slow. As I had intended, the driver saw me. The blonde head swiveled as I approached and a voice called to me over the roar of the idling motor. The voice belonged to a young woman. A frightened young woman.

"Are you Caitlin?"

"Yeah," I called back. "Who are you?"

"Shrew," she said. She looked back nervously over her shoulder. "It's no good. They're onto me," she called, her voice breaking. Frightened? Amend that to terrified. "I'm going to throw some things in the dumpster by the highway. Get them when it's clear. I'll call you later. And don't come after me. Just do what I ask. Please."

"But —"

The screech of tires cut me off. Fairly leaping off the asphalt, the little Bug went careening out of the parking lot, and as it passed the large metal dumpster, I saw a flash of white as Shrew tossed something in. For my part, I beat a hasty retreat back to Murphy's and crouched down behind the battered Honda Civic. Not a moment too soon, either. A big, late-model American car — a Buick Century or an Olds Cutlass by its lines — rocketed into the Donut Stop, slowed for a heartbeat or two, then

7

hurtled toward the exit driveway. I had one fleeting glimpse of two male profiles — one bearded and sharp-featured, one bushy-haired and blunt-featured — as the car shot past. I squinted, and was barely able to make out the first three letters of the license plate — BRY. Then, with a shower of sparks from a low-slung muffler, the bigger car disappeared into the darkness toward Victoria.

I dithered for a moment, tempted to follow, but recalled what the young woman had said. Who was I to argue? After all — I had been hired to retrieve the package. Nothing more.

Still, I crouched behind the Civic in the shadows, hesitating. Even though no one had popped out of the bushes, I still didn't like this one bit. Packages that can't be delivered in the light of day, by UPS or Federal Express or even the postal service, usually have nasty, embarrassing, or incriminating contents. I had already decided that if the package contained drugs or money, this was a game I did not want to play. Frightened or not, Shrew would have to find someone else.

I walked over to my car, took the flashlight out of the glove compartment, and headed for the highway. A cold finger of wind found its way down my collar, and my teeth began to chatter and I hurried over to the dumpster. Shining my light into its depths, I discovered to my dismay that it was far from empty. A layer of garbage — bagged and unbagged — lay two feet deep on the floor. I clamped my nostrils shut and tried to breathe through my mouth. Then, quickly, before I had a chance to change my mind, I heaved a leg up and over and let myself down into the smelly depths. Things I refused to imagine squished underfoot, and I resolutely told myself not to think about maggots. Or rats. The package Shrew had tossed in was right in the corner, and seemed to be a coarsely woven cotton sack. I bent and picked it up with my free hand, and as my fingers closed over the drawstring, something inside seemed to squirm.

"Jesus Christ!" I exclaimed, dropping the drawstring and leaping backwards. Shining the flashlight on the sack, I saw that it was indeed squirming. "Oh, shit," I whispered. Now what? I swallowed, gingerly reached for the drawstring, and pulled the sack toward me. It was heavier than I expected — maybe five pounds. And now I had no choice but to pick it up. Holding the sack at arm's length, I waded through the garbage back to the side of the dumpster, then dropped my load outside. Vaulting out, I landed on the asphalt beside it. Fortunately it wasn't squirming. I felt encouraged. Maybe it hadn't squirmed at all. Maybe it had been my imagination. I shone the light on it, and to my dismay, the sack gave a convulsive heave.

I estimated the distance between the dumpster and the trunk of my car to be about fifty feet. I could be there in five or six seconds. Grabbing the sack by the drawstring, I held it as far away from my body as I could. Then I hustled myself over to my car, fishing the keys out of my pocket as I went. I opened the trunk lid, heaved the bag inside, and was just preparing to slam the lid down when I heard a sound. From the sack.

"Maair," a voice said mournfully, hopelessly.

"What?" I asked in amazement.

"Meeeaair," it reiterated, with a great deal more feeling this time.

9

"No," I said, my numb fingers wrestling with the sack's drawstring. "It can't be."

But it was. As soon as I had loosened the drawstring, a head popped out. A cat's head. A small, striped tabby head, which swiveled in the direction of my voice. But there was something terribly wrong. I bent closer, an atavistic dread gripping me. What in hell had happened to its eyes? With a cry, I stuffed the cat back into the sack, slammed the trunk, leaped into my car, and burned rubber out of the parking lot and onto the highway.

Chapter 2

I stood in the cold wind, the cat in the sack clutched in one arm, and pounded on Gray Ng's front door.

"Be home," I prayed, my teeth chattering. "And please hurry up."

A light went on somewhere inside, and I heard footsteps. I knew I was being inspected through the little peephole in the massive oak door, and I stepped back a little to let the porch light shine on me. I heard locks being turned, and finally the door opened.

Gray stood there in jeans and a navy sweatshirt.

Her two enormous brindled Great Danes — the girls — flanked her. "Caitlin," she said, as pleasantly as though I had dropped in for afternoon tea. "Come in."

"I'm sorry to wake you," I said as she closed and locked the door behind me.

"Oh, you didn't," she said matter-of-factly. "I wasn't asleep. I was working on a report for a client." She smiled, motioning me into the living room. "Animal psychologists and detectives have at least one thing in common — late hours."

"I'm certainly glad of that," I told her. "At this hour of the night I couldn't think of anywhere else to go with this."

"What do you have there?" she asked.

I looked over at the girls sitting alertly by Gray's armchair, and visions of a cat and dog circus flitted through my mind. One of the girls yawned, showing a remarkable array of sharp white teeth. "Humor me on this one," I told her. "Let's go into the bathroom."

Gray's eyes followed mine to the girls. "Very well," she said, amusement in her voice.

In the bathroom, once I had made certain that the door was firmly closed, I set the sack down on the countertop. "I think you'd better take it from here."

Gray untied the sack and looked inside. I heard the forceful exhalation of her breath, but other than that, she gave no reaction. She gently lifted the cat out of the sack, stood him on the counter, and kneeled down so they were on eye level. Or would have been if the cat could have seen anything. In the bright light of the bathroom, I could see that the little cat was a classic brown tabby, with a wonderful

12

dark M on his forehead. I could also see the dried residue of some whitish substance that had oozed out from between his eyelids, and some wet, sticky-looking, greenish-yellow gelatinous stuff that looked like pus. Both eyes were gummed shut. I felt like throwing up. Gray petted him, and the cat relaxed visibly, finally sitting on the counter with his feet tucked neatly underneath him. Unbelievably, he began to purr. His head drooped a little, and he sighed gustily.

Gray straightened up. "Jeoffrey," she said definitively.

The cat raised his head to the sound of her voice.

She reached down and petted him again, and he resumed his rumbling purr.

"We can leave him here for a few moments," she told me. "I want to move him to one of the large cages in my back room. Come on. You can make coffee for us while I get his cage ready."

In Gray's tiny, neat kitchen, I ground the coffee and turned on the gas underneath the kettle, not doubting for a moment that Gray now knew the cat's name was Jeoffrey. How did she know? Well of course, he'd told her. I might have doubted anyone else, but not Gray. After all, how many people did I know who had been fired from their jobs as veterinary assistants for being witches? As I recalled, her boss had called her "a damned Asian witch." Well at least he had been two-thirds accurate.

It was only this past year that Gray had taken my suggestion and opened her animal psychology practice. She'd been talking to the animals for years, I told her, so why not try to make some money at it? Now three local vets referred their behavior problems to Gray. She had had clients as diverse as a Burmese python who persistently, and too enthusiastically, constricted its owner's lover; a Scottie who went berserk and bit ankles whenever anyone walked over a certain floorboard; and a lilac point Siamese cat who routinely hid her owner's brokerage statements.

Gray appeared at my elbow as I was pouring the coffee into mugs. "Come," she said. "We'll go in the back and sit with Jeoffrey. He needs to hear friendly human voices."

"The girls?" I inquired warily.

"They're already there," she said.

And indeed they were, I saw as we went down the hall and into the back bedroom Gray kept for her resident clients. There were two large floor-to-ceiling cages in the room, each containing an old armchair, a litter pan, a raised platform with water and kibble dishes, a carpeted cat tree, and a high ledge. The doors which led to the outside runs were closed at this hour of the night. In front of one of the cages lay the girls, and just inside, on a mat, lay Jeoffrey, pressed as close to the big dogs as the mesh would allow. Gray took a seat at her desk and pulled a yellow writing tablet out of a drawer. I sat at the side of the desk in an easy chair sipping my coffee. Gray pressed a button on the stereo beside her desk, and a dissonant, yet strangely pleasant music filled the room.

"Kitaro," she said. "Cats like New Age music. This is the 'Silk Road,' I believe." She looked up at me for just a moment; I saw the pain in her eyes, the flip side of her gift.

Something from one of my university literature courses flitted through my mind: *If we had keen*

*vision and feeling, it would be like hearing the grass
grow and the squirrel's heartbeat, and we should die
of the roar that lies on the other side of silence.* I
always wondered if Gray heard that roar.

Her eyes as flat and opaque as a seal's, Gray
looked off into a distance only she could see, and in
that moment I knew as surely as I have ever known
anything that I sat in the presence of a very old soul.
For that instant I believed in reincarnation, and I
almost understood what my friend was. Then I
blinked, and the instant was gone. Gray was just a
small Vietnamese woman in a worn navy sweatshirt,
writing by lamplight. And I an over-imaginative fool.

"I'll have a vet come and check the cat in the
morning," she said. "I'll do what I can for him in the
meantime. Also, he has a badly infected sore on his
arm. I'll get the vet to take care of that, too." She
sat back in her chair and looked at me. "So how did
you acquire him?"

I took a deep breath, and told her as much of the
story as I knew. Ruefully, I had to admit it wasn't
much. "I'm not sure what comes next," I said. "I
guess Shrew will call me and I'll hand him over."

Gray put down her pen and shook her head. "It
won't be that easy, I fear."

"Oh?"

"Surely you know that Jeoffrey is a pawn in
someone's game."

I sighed. "I'm trying not to think about it.
Whatever's going on is no business of mine."

"Ah," Gray said meaningfully.

I refused to rise to the bait. I yawned, despite the
coffee. "Gray, if I don't go home to bed, I'm going to
pass out and slide under your desk." I handed over

one of my crisp hundred-dollar bills. "This is an installment on his — on Jeoffrey's — care." I stood up, stretching. "Thanks for helping."

Gray walked me to the front door. The girls, I noted, had decided to stay behind with Jeoffrey. "Caitlin," Gray said, stepping out onto the porch with me. "You must take care with this one."

I turned to look at her, surprised. Gray never gave me advice. "Well, okay," I assured her, too startled to ask for elucidation.

"Good," she said, nodding as if we had sealed a bargain. "Very good. Now go home."

* * * * *

I pulled into my driveway just after two a.m., parked, and simply sat there, unable to summon up the energy to move. It was late, and my drive through the darkness to Gray's with the cat in the sack crying in the trunk had exhausted my store of emotional energy. What would become of the cat, I wondered. Worse yet, what had happened to it? To Jeoffrey, if that was indeed its name. I didn't want to think about it, but I found I couldn't help myself. Who would mistreat an animal so?

I sighed, and dragged my weary body up the steps and into my house. The living room was cold and dark, and I decided that late though the hour might be, I needed light, fire, and music. I snapped on the table lamps on either end of the sofa, and knelt on the hearth, preparing to build a fire. After two tries, the kindling and newspaper finally caught, and in another moment, greedy little orange flames were lapping at the cedar logs I laid in the firebasket. I dusted off my hands and stood up.

"Mrraannk?" my portly gray cat, Repo, commented from behind my favorite overstuffed chair.

"I know what you're up to over there, you sharp-clawed ingrate," I told him. Repo was in disfavor, having recently taken to giving himself manicures on the back of the aforementioned chair.

He peered out at me with slit-eyed feline indifference.

"Listen, buster," I said, going over to explain a few of the facts of life to him. Emulating Gray, I kneeled down beside him and looked him in the eye. "You live the life of Riley compared to the cat in the sack. You're in feline Lotus Land. So stop complaining. And stop destroying the furniture."

"Mrraaff," he said, plainly intending to ignore my comments.

As I popped a tape into the cassette player, Repo strode by, flicking his tail in a feline version of The Bird. "Damn it," I said to myself, regretting my display of pique. This was the first time in two days he had emerged from the box of rags in the depths of my closet. What did he get for his efforts at sociability? A lecture. Caitlin, you are an insensitive harpy, I told myself. Give the cat a break.

"Hey, Repo," I called after him. "C'mon back. I'm sorry."

He turned to regard me once, with his When Hell Freezes Over, Sister look, then flicked his tail again and continued on his way to the bedroom.

"Damned cat," I muttered. To tell the truth, I was more than a little worried about him. For the past three days, he had spurned his breakfast and his afternoon kibble offering. More alarming, the level in his water bowl seemed to be the same. Did I have a sick cat on my hands? I thought of the astronomical fees vets charged, and shuddered. Well, I reminded myself, at least I had nine of the crisp one-hundred-dollar bills left. And the hundred I had forked over to Gray was going to be replaced by Ms. Shrew — I'd see to that. After all, my fees were two hundred and fifty dollars a day *plus* expenses.

I poured myself a Scotch and hauled the rocking chair over to the fire. Wrapping myself in my Grandma's heather-colored mohair blanket, I sat sipping, staring, and listening to Handel's "Water Music."

I looked at my watch. Quarter to three on a late October morning in the Pacific Northwest. It would soon be winter — our least pleasant season. We on Vancouver Island congratulate ourselves that we live in the best of all possible climates, and for most of the year this is certainly true. Lately, however, the winters seemed to be getting harsher — why, last winter we had *snow*. Perhaps what the geologists tell us is true — the ice age cometh. One scientific opinion I read recently hypothesized that the ice age was about seventy years overdue, and that the only thing holding it off was our burning of wood and fossil fuels. This combustion created a layer of particulate matter and CO_2 that blanketed the earth and kept the heat in, so the argument went. It seemed logical to me. And another good reason for having a fire tonight. Burn more wood: keep the ice age at bay. And the jackals too.

I finished my Scotch and reached over to set the

18

glass on the brick hearth. Shrew. What an unlikely name. Someone's idea of romance, no doubt. Probably a bunch of students, "liberating" animals from one of the university's labs. That sort of thing happened from time to time, despite the fact that the university told us repeatedly that no experiments — well, maybe a few benign learning experiments in the Psychology Department — were performed on animals. Ha. Tell that to Repo. When members of the student Animal Liberation Corps liberated Repo three years ago, he was almost dead. Apparently he had been used in one of the Psych Department's "benign" experiments, then forgotten. Over the Christmas holidays the animal-lab keeper had gone on a two-week vacation and had made no arrangements for the care of his furry charges. Nine of the twelve cats were dead by the time the ALC got to them, and two had to be euthanized. Repo was the only survivor of the university's benign use of animals. I wondered idly if Shrew was a member of the ALC in new clothes — student animal activists who had graduated and gone on to challenge bigger bad guys. Was the university up to its old tricks again? I doubted it, considering the media coverage of the dead cats in the psych lab. But if not the university, who then? I supposed I'd find out.

I wondered if my tenants knew anything about this. Malcolm and Yvonne, a pair of blond, expatiate Australians who run the local health food store and cafe, rent the upstairs of my house. Their establishment near the university was a favorite haunt of students. I made a mental note to talk to them before they took off in the morning to fricassee the shiitake or parboil the nori or whatever it was

19

they needed to do for that day's veggie special. Now don't misunderstand me — I'm not a total barbarian. Or a blockhead. I realize that there may be some health benefits associated with eating a vegetarian diet. But my main quibble with vegetarian cooking is that it's such a dangerous occupation. It requires far too much dexterity with sharp instruments. Malcolm is deadly with a cleaver — he can have a carrot sliced, diced, and in the soup pot in the time it takes me to find the knife. Brrr — all that chopping scares me to death. Who wants to have to study to be a Ninja master just to cook dinner? I've learned to handle a can opener, and that's the extent of the bladed weapons I intend to master. Thank the Lord for fast food outlets and delis.

I must have dozed off, because when I opened my eyes the fire had died away. But somehow, the eyes I looked out of were not my own. I had awakened in a large, dimly lit room, and the colors my human eyes should have seen were nothing but shades of gray. I knew, without knowing how I knew, that it was dark outside. I looked around, puzzled. I seemed to be in a box about one foot square. In front of me was a grid of metal. I pressed up against it, but it refused to budge. Then it came to me — I was in a cage, and beside me, below and on top of me were rows of other cages. I opened my nostril and the smell of my fellows flooded in — smells of urine and feces, of sweat and vomit. Smells of despair and terror. A few of us moaned in uneasy sleep, but I could sense that most were awake. Awake and terrified of something in the room with us. The thing we feared most, more than we feared the men-with-things-that-hurt. I squealed, as did several of the others — a feeble show

20

of defiance — as in the shadows I saw the monster begin to grow. I heard its voice, smelled its breath, felt —

My empty glass hit the floor with a clatter, breaking the spell. I awoke fully, in my own body, in my living room. The fire was out and I was stiff and chilled. I pulled the mohair blanket around myself, and wondered just whose mind I had inhabited for those few dream moments. And the presence in the room where I had been imprisoned, that awful, malevolent *thing*. What in hell had that been? What was I to make of this? In the murky gray light of dawn, I decided that I felt too dispirited to dwell on such things. Sufficient unto the day were the puzzles thereof. And this day hadn't even begun yet. Tomorrow. I'd think about it tomorrow.

Feeling fragile, I got up out of my chair, folding the blanket. Fluffing it a little, I laid it on the floor behind my armchair. Just in case Repo needed to take a nap in the middle of his next manicure. Grandma Maedhbh would understand.

In my bedroom, I didn't bother to undress. I just kicked off my Reeboks, and wrapped myself in my down comforter.

"Night, Repo," I called to him in the bowels of my closet.

Only silence answered me.

MONDAY

Chapter 3

When my clock radio trilled into life just before 7:00 a.m. I wasn't certain for a moment if I were alive or dead. "Arrk," I managed finally, struggling to escape from the coils of my comforter. When my feet hit the icy floor, I realized at once that I was alive. A masterful job of deduction.

In the bathroom, I whiffled and whuffled as I splashed cold water on my face and ran a brush through my hair. The remnants of a dream wafted through my mind, evanescent as mist, and I frowned. Coffee first, I told myself. Shower next. Behind me in the bedroom some adenoidal young tenor assured me that my kiss was on his list of the best things in life. Then the seven o'clock news began.

"Another fatal accident on the Pat Bay Highway," the announcer read. "Provincial Police report that at about one o'clock this morning, a red Volkswagen Bug crashed through the guard rail and fell to the rocks, fatally injuring the car's driver, a young woman of about twenty-five. It appears that alcohol was involved. The identity of the driver is being withheld pending notification of next of kin. Police ask anyone witnessing the accident to call the Saanich office of the BCPP."

I froze, hairbrush in hand. Oh come off it, Caitlin, I told myself. How many red VWs could there be in Victoria? Hundreds, maybe. Well, dozens anyhow. Still, the coincidence bothered me.

I wandered into the kitchen, got the coffee perking, and phoned upstairs to Malcolm and Yvonne's. No answer. Presumably a pressing appointment with the ratatouille had taken them off to the cafe early. I'd have to drop in on them later.

Yawning, I retrieved the newspaper from the front porch and carried it into the kitchen. As I poured coffee, I looked outside, checking the weather. The morning was a little foggy, but after peering at the sky, I concluded this was the kind of fog that would burn off by midday. We would probably have a beautiful afternoon — a Technicolor sort of day that only occurs on the coast, a day when everything sparkles, and the sky is such an impossible shade of blue that you can hardly bear it. Days like that bring out the gardener in all us Victorians, and even I vowed to go outside later and commune with nature.

Maybe I'd rake up the leaves in my side yard. The two massive oaks were already bare, but my maple, which had turned a fiery red-gold at first frost two weeks ago, still stood proudly bearing its bounty of leaves like individual flames. And the apple tree — home for family after family of robins — had a bumper crop of apples. I really should pick them, I thought. Make a pie. Or some apple butter. Be domestic. I snorted — who was I kidding? I'd be doing well to get the leaves raked.

The phone rang and I answered it with no great interest, my mind on my afternoon's chores.

"Caitlin Reece?"

"Yes."

"Did you read this morning's paper?" an aggressive female voice asked.

I always discourage telephone games like this. The caller is usually some weirdo with a burning desire to know the color of your pubic hair. "What do you want?" I asked naturally, on the off chance that this *was* a client.

"We're friends of Shrew," the voice informed me.

"So?"

There was silence for a moment. Then the voice exploded in my ear. "She's dead, dammit. Dead! Doesn't that affect you at all? She was your client, for God's sake. Not that you did her any bloody good."

I held the phone out away from my ear as the voice vilified me. Shrew dead? So she had been the driver of the wrecked VW, just as I had suspected. Damn. Why was I cursed with knowing these things? But the wacko on the phone had to be discouraged.

"Listen, you," I told her shortly. "You may well

be friends of Shrew, but my dealings with her are confidential. They have nothing to do with you. And just for the record, of course I'm sorry she's dead — if indeed she is."

"You're cool, I'll give you that," the voice continued nastily, "but you need to get a few things straight. Shrew may have hired you but we all made the decision together, and we all put up the money together. Ten one-hundred-dollar bills. Shrew was representing us."

I thought this over. "Go on."

The voice had become a little more reasonable. "You have something that belongs to us."

"Maybe," I equivocated.

"Don't be cute. We want the packages she gave you."

Hold on — packages? Wasn't the cat in the sack the only thing she had left for me? I closed my eyes and tried to replay Shrew's words. *I have some things* . . . Things. Not thing. Damn. The voice was right.

"Are you there?" the voice inquired testily.

"Yeah," I sighed. "Okay. We have to get together and talk. You need to prove to me that you are who you claim to be — friends of Shrew. And I need to establish for sure that she's dead."

Silence.

Then the voice asked huskily, "How will you . . . establish that?"

"I'll call the morgue. I know people there. But I have to know Shrew's real name."

A pause. Then, "Mary Shepard."

"Okay," I said. "Meet me this afternoon at the Inner Harbor. Where the float planes land."

28

"I can't. It's too public."

That took the wind out of my sails. Too public? Who was she — Barbara Bush? Fergie? Mata Hari? "The gardens at the art gallery should be pretty private about two o'clock this time of year. And that's my last offer."

She conferred with someone. "All right. Be sure to bring both packages.

"One thing at a time," I told her. "I said we'd talk. So we'll talk."

I could hear muffled voices as she consulted again. "That's okay for now," she said. "But don't get any ideas abut keeping what Shrew gave you."

I thought about the enormous vet bill the cat in the sack must be running. "Nothing could be farther from my mind."

I hung up the phone and ran a hand through my hair. I needed to shower, talk to Malcolm and Yvonne, go to my bank, and . . . what else? Suddenly, I remembered. Today was the day I had planned to take Repo to the vet. But first things first. I checked my watch — not quite eight o'clock. How early were garbage dumpsters emptied, anyhow? I had a feeling I'd better hurry. Racing back to the bedroom, I pulled on a pair of jeans and a sweatshirt, jammed my feet into my oldest pair of running shoes, and grabbed my windbreaker.

* * * * *

Back at the Donut Stop, all was quiet. Was it my imagination though, or was the dumpster in a slightly different place from where it had sat last night? Was I already too late? Would I be doomed to pursue this

29

particular load of debris across the province like the Flying Dutchman? I pulled my MG to a stop, got out, and before I could think better of it, hopped inside. No indeed, the dumpster hadn't been emptied. If anything, it was at least half a foot fuller than it had been last night. I breathed through my mouth and looked resolutely ahead. Don't look down, I told myself as my foot broke through the plastic of a green garbage bag and I sank to my ankles in cold ooze. Finally I was there — the far right-hand corner of the dumpster. But what was I looking for? Gingerly, I pulled bags of garbage aside, suppressing a gag. There. A large white envelope. I picked it up by one corner. It was Tyvek, that blend of paper and plastic fiber that was water repellant, and nearly indestructible. I held it by one corner and looked at it.

CAITLIN REECE, someone had scrawled hastily across the front. I thought again about Shrew, of the fear in her eyes.

"Okay, Mary," I said softly. "I've got both of them now."

*　*　*　*　*

At the McDonald's on the highway I used the sink in the ladies' room to scrub my hands and feet. My shoes were beyond hope, so I abandoned them in the trash bin and marched barefoot back to my car. At the drive-through, I ordered an Egg McMuffin, juice, and coffee, with only a twinge of guilt. One of these days real soon I'm going to get a cholesterol check. Malcolm and Yvonne have almost convinced me to do it. But maybe not this week, I decided. When my

30

breakfast arrived, I toasted my HDL with a flourish, and chug-a-lugged my orange juice.

"Among them be it," I intoned, uttering my grandmother's favorite all-purpose fatalistic saying.

I pulled into a parking place, ate the Egg McMuffin in about a minute, then considered the Tyvek envelope. My Swiss Army knife made short work of the fabric, and I cautiously looked inside. Two rolls of film, held together with a rubber band. Nothing more threatening than that. What had I expected anyhow, I asked myself, feeling foolish. An asp?

I sipped the last of my coffee and looked thoughtfully out at the gray autumn sky. One fleeing woman, one maimed cat, and two rolls of film. What was going on here? I couldn't put the first two parts of the puzzle in their places, but I knew someone who could help me with the last two. I suddenly wanted very much to see what was on those rolls of film.

* * * * *

"Lester!" a girl with a topknot of red spiky hair called over her shoulder. "He's in the back," she explained to me, returning to the camera she was disemboweling. I studied her covertly. This was the first time I had ever seen really red hair. I mean, it was *crimson*. And how did she get it to stand up like that? She looked like some exotic bird. A hoopoe, maybe. I had just about decided I was becoming an old fogey when Lester appeared in the doorway.

I hadn't seen him for about six months, but he looked just the same — tousled sandy hair, friendly blue eyes, aviator glasses. Neatly ironed blue cotton shirt, clean jeans. Lester is a nice guy — I was glad I had been able to rescue him last year from the influence of his criminal companions and point him down the straight and narrow again. Even if he had almost gotten killed in the process.

"Caitlin!" he said, his face lighting up. I felt touched. He was actually glad to see me. I wasn't sure how he would feel once he had had time to think things over. After all, I *had* blackmailed him into helping me with that case. Well, it was heartening to see that he bore me no ill will. "How are you?" He took me by the arm and guided me over to a display of photography books.

"I'm okay. How are you doing, Lester? Still in Journalism?"

He nodded happily. "Yeah. I'm editor of the paper this term. And I got a promotion here at the camera shop. I'm assistant manager — evenings and weekends. It pays another two dollars an hour," he said, lowering his voice modestly.

Crimson Crest glanced over at us curiously. Well, let her think what she would. Having an older woman admirer wouldn't hurt Lester's image.

"Er, do you have," he cleared his throat, "something for me to do? I meant it when I said that if you ever needed me to help you again, I would." He looked a little embarrassed, and I smiled. Faithful Lester. I had almost gotten him killed, and he wanted to help. Well, I had something nice and safe for him to do.

"As a matter of fact, I do need your help." I pulled the two film containers out of my pocket. "Can I come by for these at one o'clock or so?"

"No problem," he assured me. "Will a proof sheet be all right?"

"I think so. Oh, listen, Lester. Do them yourself, okay?"

He swallowed, and pushed his glasses back up on his nose. "Okay. They're . . . important, aren't they?" he asked, smelling adventure.

I saw no reason to lie. Lester was one of the few people who knew what I really did for a living. "I'm not sure yet. But for your own good, assume they are."

"I will," he said seriously. "You can count on me. I'll be here until two."

I patted him on the shoulder. "Thanks, Lester. See you then."

* * * * *

As I pulled into my driveway and hurried up the steps to my house, I realized rather grumpily that perhaps I *wasn't* going to get the yard raked today. Nor the apples picked. It's one of the least understood laws of physics that time spent enjoying oneself always passes faster than time spent in drudgery. I'm certain that an hour spent in pleasure has about forty-five minutes, while an hour spent in toil — working one's taxes, or suffering in the dentist's chair, or cleaning house — has seventy-five. Or more. Ah well, the leaves could wait for another day.

I poked my head into the closet on my way to the bathroom.

"What's up?" I called to Repo. Darn it all, I missed his furry presence. "All right for you," I told

33

him. "It's off to Dr. Neely when I get back. Remember how much you liked it last time? You got a big fat needle in the butt."

Still no answer. My attempt at terrifying the cat into cooperation had plainly fallen on deaf ears. I've noticed that about cats — they hear only what they want to hear. Repo has me convinced that his auditory nerve cannot pick up the word *no*, even when uttered very loudly, and sometimes next to his ear; however, that same nerve can pick up the sound of a can opener at one hundred paces. Curious, isn't it?

I trotted into the bathroom and turned on the shower. What *was* the matter with that cat? An obscure disease? A feline mid-life crisis? Ennui? Angst? I shook my head. Emma Neely would find out.

Under the water, I hummed a few bars from "Sheep May Safely Graze" and thought about my upcoming meeting with the owner of the insistent telephone voice. I didn't like it, and I was sure I wouldn't like its owner. In fact there wasn't much I did like about this case so far — the late night I had just spent freezing my hindquarters off on Saanich Highway, the cat I had had to rescue, the vet bill he was no doubt incurring, the garbage I had had to wade through. Damn it anyhow, this wasn't why I had gone into business for myself. I could have had this much fun working in the Crown Prosecutor's office.

Well, maybe not quite.

I shut off the water and, stepping out of the tub, wrapped myself in a fluffy towel. Wiping the steam off the mirror, I plugged in the hair dryer and waved it around a little. Growing quickly bored with all this primping, I shut off the dryer, brushed my half-dry hair vigorously, cleaned my teeth, and then glanced at myself in the mirror, grimacing. My glassy Doppelganger grimaced back — a middle-aged woman with eyes neither green nor gray, hair neither red nor brown, and a mouth that wanted to smile but found too little to smile about these days. Caitlin Reece, about to turn forty, self-employed, perennially broke, voice of the voiceless, defender of the weak, champion of lost causes, final hope for those whom the system had chewed up and spit out.

I knew how those lost souls felt, for I, too, was a victim of the system. My seven years spent as an attorney in the Crown Prosecutor's office had been too much for me. Muggers, pimps, rapists, murderers, wife-beaters, child molesters — they slipped through the grasp of the justice system with ridiculous ease. For every one we put behind bars, three walked away. And they walked away laughing at us. It was the Marc Bergeron trial — the man responsible for the disappearance, rape, and murder of six-year-old Annie Graves — that finally broke me. He copped an insanity plea and got life in a cushy institution up-island. Annie Graves got a funeral one rainy Sunday in April. And I got smart. I resigned from the CP's office the day Bergeron's lawyer pleaded him crazy. Because he was no crazier than you or I. He was evil, and that's a whole different story. But I knew that if I had to sit across the table from many more Marc Bergerons, I would soon be genuinely, certifiably nuts. I was afraid I'd slip into a warm bath one night and open a vein. Or cuddle up to the open door of the gas oven. So I quit. And I've never regretted it. But what does trouble me from time to time is the nagging doubt that what I'm doing now may be just as fruitless. So I manage to help a few people — so what? What does that mean, anyhow, on a cosmic scale? Most of the time I feel like King Canute, standing on the beach, commanding the waves to stop. We all know what happened to him, right? Right. He ruined his best boots.

I hurried into the bedroom, pulled on a pair of clean levis, a pale yellow cotton turtleneck, and threaded a braided leather belt through the belt loops. From a shoebox in my closet, I took my .357 Magnum, checked the load, and clipped its holster to the back of my jeans. My Harris Tweed blazer draped quite nicely, I thought, checking myself out in the full-length mirror. The gun made nary a bulge. I laced on a pair of well broken-in Reeboks, batted my eyelashes girlishly at my reflection, and ran out of the house.

* * * * *

Disagreeable Voice was late. I had already toured the art gallery's sunken gardens twice, admiring the Japanese touches — the miniature Oriental stone temples, the bamboo bridge over the streamlet, the bonsai. I had sniffed the last roses and attempted again to distinguish the azaleas from the camellias with no luck. I admit it — I'm a horticultural idiot. I looked up at the sky which had become gray and overcast, ending the promise of a bright, sunny afternoon. So much for my yard-raking plans. A contingent of fat raindrops splatted down on the camellia (or azalea) leaves I was inspecting, and I retreated to the gallery's open doors. Plunking myself down on one of the stone benches, I feigned interest in a nearby Australian tree fern.

Actually, I was thinking of the photo proof sheet I had picked up from Lester. Most of the shots had been taken indoors, and showed a series of out-of-focus blobs that seemed to be animals. In some cases, one pair of hands was holding the animal, while other hands were busy doing something to it; in other cases, the animal was restrained, and only one pair of hands was in evidence. There were two shots, much clearer and crisper, of a man with a sybaritic face and a dark, neatly trimmed beard standing beside a car, talking to the driver. The car's license plate was visible. It read CHOKE. What did it all mean? Apart from the fact that someone needed photography lessons, I had no idea.

"Caitlin Reece?" a quiet voice said.

I turned. In the gallery's doorway stood a smallish, fair-haired woman in an oyster-colored raincoat, worn open over navy pants and a fisherman-knit sweater. I rose to my feet. The watery sun chose that moment to shine through the high gallery windows, and suddenly it seemed that all the light in the dreary afternoon was concentrated onto that small figure. Her fair hair seemed to glow — a lambent halo neither gold nor silver, but an intermediate shade all its own. And her light eyes — not the blue I had first thought, but a pale gray — seemed opalescent, the color of clouds scudding across winter seas. I knew I was staring, but I was unable to help myself. I felt as though I had been punched just under the heart. She held out her hand, and when I took it, I had a hard time remembering what I was supposed to do with it. I blinked, suspended for a moment in space and time, trying witlessly to function.

"Yes," I said finally, remembering her question. "I'm Caitlin Reece." Speech helped. See — I had even remembered who I was. Wonderful progress was being made. With difficulty, I managed to corral a few more of my wandering wits. "But you're not the woman I talked to on the phone." I was positive of that.

"No," she said, turning the corners of her mouth down in an embarrassed smile. "That was Judith. She's a bit of a hothead, I'm afraid." She looked up at me, gray eyes serious. "She's also angry and filled with guilt. We all are. We let Mary go off into danger — some of us against our better judgment." She looked into the distance, then quickly back at me. "Did you find out what you said you would?"

"Oh, er, yes. I called my friend at the morgue. She confirmed it."

"Damn. Somehow, I hoped . . ."

"I'm sorry," I said automatically.

She took a deep breath and looked at me. "We desperately need your help. I'm afraid we're in way over our heads this time. Please don't reject us because Judith antagonized you. Can we start over somehow?"

"I don't know," I said honestly, trying hard not to look at those disturbing eyes. "I don't know who you are. And I have no idea what your problem is. Shrew — sorry, Mary — hired me to take some packages. I did that. But I don't know what else she, or you, had in mind. It's possible that I might not be able to help. And — I'll be honest with you — from what I've seen of this case, I'm not sure I want to."

She blinked quickly, and I saw that despite her

facade of composure, she was anxious and frightened. "Thank you for your honesty. And of course, what you decide is up to you." She smiled a little crookedly. "But you're wrong about not being able to help us. I'm positive you can."

I raised an eyebrow. Such confidence was flattering, but I needed something a little more definite to go on. "Do you have a reason for all this optimism?"

"Yes, of course." She looked around apprehensively. "Could we . . . go somewhere. I really don't feel comfortable talking here."

"Now listen," I said, aware that my exasperation was evident. "This place was all right with your friend."

"I'm sorry," she said. "But there's a much better place to talk not far from here — that little restaurant catty-corner from the Executive House. Victoria Jane's. It has the virtue of being dark and quiet. Do you know it?"

I nodded.

She looked at her watch. "It's two-thirty. I have to stop and make a phone call. Let's meet there about three."

* * * * *

I took another sip of my J & B, and from the sanctuary of my dark, quiet booth in Victoria Jane's, looked at the doorway for about the twentieth time. It was now three-thirty and the lady with the gray eyes had still not appeared. Well, I'd give her until four, and then I intended to go home and take Repo to the vet.

I thought about my meeting with her in the garden, and just for a moment I felt again the disorientation, the sense of wonder I had felt when I looked at her. The lyrics from "My Heart Stood Still" began to go through my head.

I snorted. Quoting lyrics from love songs was a particularly bad sign, I told myself. It preceded things like sending flowers, writing bad poetry, and baying at the moon. So she had pretty gray eyes. So what? She probably snored, or liked Hockey Night in Canada, or couldn't stand cats. Some fatal flaw. Get a grip, Reece.

"Sorry." Gray Eyes slipped onto the seat across the table from me. "It was a long phone call."

"Let me guess," I said. "The woman who called me didn't want you to come here. She told you that you were wasting your time, and suggested other more direct methods of getting what you folks want from me. She even offered to try some."

She looked guilty and I knew I had been right.

"I didn't think it would work," she said, looking at me appraisingly. "All right. We —" A waiter arrived, interrupting her, and she ordered a dry sherry. When he was out of earshot, she continued. "I'll tell you what Mary would have told you. I assume she did say she'd be in touch with you?"

I nodded.

The sherry arrived, and she took a healthy swallow.

"Before we get started, tell me who recommended me to Mary."

"Tonia Konig," she said, putting her glass down carefully on the table.

I sat back, surprised. Tonia was one-half of my

last employer team. A professor of political philosophy, an outspoken feminist and advocate of non-violence, Tonia had reluctantly hired me to retrieve some incriminating letters which had been stolen from her home. Letters written to her by Val Frazier, Victoria's most glamorous television news anchorwoman, and possibly its most closeted lesbian. And letters written by Tonia to Val. Tonia had disliked me on sight, but we eventually arrived at an uneasy accord. Retrieving the letters had cost me several broken ribs, a fair amount of blood, and almost lost me my life. For Tonia, the affair had meant a realignment of lifelong beliefs. I was touched and flattered that she had recommended me.

"A good reference," I said, taking a quick drink to cover old emotions.

"Tonia told all three of us abut you," she said softly. "She told us the kinds of things you do, and a little about how you helped her. We agreed to hire you to be . . . backup for Mary. She was to get in touch with you if she ran into trouble at Living World. I only wish she hadn't waited so long to make the contact." She looked directly at me. "I'll tell you anything you want to know. How do we . . . do this?"

"Simple. Tell me what you need me to do, and I'll tell you if I think I can do it."

"All right. My name is Alison Bell. The woman you spoke with — the woman who antagonized you so — is Judith Hadley. And Mary Shepard was the woman who hired you. Shrew. Along with two other people — Liz McLaren and Ian Burns — we form the local branch of an organization called Ninth Life." She paused and looked at me.

I shrugged. "Sorry. I've never heard of it."

"We're animal rights advocates. Ninth Life is a national organization. Well, an international organization, really. But it's called by different names in Britain and West Germany." She paused again.

Impressive. "I haven't heard of your group, but I do know about animal rights organizations. I saw some television footage about the treatment of dogs in labs. Is it your group that lets lab animals loose and protests outside medical schools in gorilla suits — that sort of thing?"

She grimaced. "Among other activities. Groups like ours haven't received very good treatment at the hands of the media, I'm afraid. And we deserve a lot of the bad press we've gotten. But sometimes trespassing, breaking and entering, or theft are the only ways to get what we want."

Tell me about it. I understood her plight only too well. "So what exactly is it you want?"

She bent forward, gray eyes intent. "Evidence, Miss Reece. Proof. Something we can use in court and something we can show to the media. Something that will get the public's attention."

"Like the cat Shrew tossed into the dumpster? And the photos?"

"Exactly, Miss Reece."

This Miss Reece stuff had to go. "Please call me Caitlin."

"Are you any more kindly disposed toward us . . . Caitlin?" she asked softly.

I looked up from my Scotch. "Maybe. You're certainly a good public relations person."

"Thank you," she said, a small frown making parentheses between her pale eyebrows. "As I said,

42

Ninth Life is in trouble. We need someone like you to help us."

Flattery will get you almost anywhere with me. I smiled in wry amusement. "Someone like me?" I wondered which of my sterling character traits Tonia had described to Alison — my cool-headedness under stress, my sangfroid in the face of danger, my awesome powers of deduction, my admirable physical prowess?

"Someone clever," she explained. "Someone discreet. Someone tough. Someone who isn't afraid to take a few licks — or give them out."

Oh, that again. So Ninth Life, too, wanted a heavy. I felt an obscure disappointment — in Tonia, in Ninth Life, and in Alison. "A thug," I said. "You want a thug."

She moved her shoulders in what might have been agreement. "In a manner of speaking, I suppose. But above all we want someone . . . steadfast. Someone who won't be frightened off."

Steadfast. I liked that. "What would this steadfast person do?"

"Take Mary's place. Get us the evidence we need. We were at our wits' end with Living World." Seeing my blank look, she explained. "That's a cosmetics manufacturing company. We've been after them for a long time — they've operated the same kind of business in three other provinces, and just when we think we've got the goods on them, they pack up and move on. They're a very slippery bunch. Mary talked us into letting her go undercover as a lab worker. She was to get photographs and video footage. And whatever other proof she could lay her hands on. She was supposed to call you if she needed help."

43

"But something went wrong."

"Yes," she agreed. "Something went very wrong." She took a deep breath. "So will you help us?"

"What is Living World doing that's so bad?" I asked. "What did Mary need proof *of?*"

"They're testing their cosmetics on animals at their so-called New Product Development establishment in Saanich. Their manufacturing plant is on the mainland," she explained. "Our beef with them is not that they're testing — although we're opposed to *any* testing on animals — but that they're doing it and lying about it."

I raised an eyebrow. "You mean they maintain that they're not?"

"Yes," she said emphatically. "They've built their entire ad campaign around the fact that they're benign. 'Cruelty-free' as the phrase goes. If we can expose them, their credibility will be zero. They'll lose their customer base. It will be the end."

I toyed with my glass, postponing the moment of reply. If people at Living World really had run Mary off the road, then they were determined to keep their lie a secret. They played very rough indeed, and I had absolutely no desire to tangle with them. On the other hand, I might well be able to do what Alison wanted without having to go toe to toe with the Living World contingent. There were back doors, after all. "Let me get this straight. You want to expose Living World — get whatever you can on them to see them put out of business, right?"

"Right."

I drummed my fingers on the table again. It sounded doable. Get in, get the evidence, get out. Heck, if I played my cards right, I might not even have to get in. Electronic breaking and entering often produced amazing results. "Okay. I'll do it."

She relaxed. "Thank you," she said. "But I want you to do something else, too. Something extra. Something for me alone. And I'll pay you for it myself." I had a feeling I knew what it was. "Ninth Life wants you to find out how to put Living World out of business. I want you to find out what happened to Mary." She closed her eyes for a moment, and when she opened them she looked grimly determined. "The police already have their minds made up about her — they think she was drinking and just ran off the road. I realize they're not likely to open an investigation unless we can give them some evidence. I'd like to change their minds. I believe someone is responsible for Mary's death. I'd like that someone to pay."

The waiter brought us another round of drinks just then, and I used the little ceremony of paying and tipping to give myself time to think. This was a new wrinkle. It made the whole project much less feasible. That kind of evidence would be tough to find. It would mean sticking my nose into places where it might get pinched. I don't like that. My ribs still ached from my last encounter with the Forces of Evil. I sighed. I was tempted in that moment to hand over the cat and the photos, refund as much of the money as I deemed fit, and walk away. Bail out. But visions of my pitiful bank balance stayed my hand. And what better prospects did I have, anyhow? No souls in distress had hammered on my door for quite a while. It was a daunting prospect. Were the downtrodden of the world learning self-reliance? Were there no more jams from which they couldn't

45

extricate themselves, puzzles they couldn't solve? Had all the dragons been slain?

Alison sat quietly, her hands wrapped around her sherry glass, waiting for my answer. Was this my fate, I wondered — to become a champion of the furry and four-legged?

"All right," I said, trying to ignore the voice of caution that urged me to chuck this whole thing and wait for a juicy insurance scam. Or take a job on a salmon boat. "I'll take the case. Or the cases, rather. In for a penny, in for a pound."

I couldn't believe I actually said that, but Alison didn't seem to mind the triteness. She put one hand briefly over mine. "Thank you, Caitlin."

From that point on, I would have walked through fire for her, because, truly, that was why I took the Ninth Life case. Because of her. So for the wrong reason, I did the right thing.

* * * * *

"The meeting is at seven tonight," she said as we stood at the door of Victoria Jane's, peering out at the lowering sky. "At Judith's. Our address is on the check I just gave you. We don't have an office. We try to keep a low profile. Our faces are better known than we'd like them to be. Judith and I and the others rent a house in James Bay. The basement and part of the first floor accommodates our printing press, library, darkroom, and so on. We live in the rest of the space." She belted her raincoat around her waist and we eyed the drizzle together. "I'm glad you said yes," she said earnestly, turning to face me.

46

"After I talk to Judith and get her cooled down, I'll introduce you. But, Caitlin . . ."

She was clearly having trouble with this. "What?"

"You can tell the others whatever you like about your investigation into Living World — after all, you'll be working for all of us. But I don't want you to tell anyone that you're working for me on Mary's death. I just . . . don't." She tilted her chin a little as if she expected an argument from me.

"That's your prerogative," I told her. "You're my employer. Part of what your money buys is my loyalty and my discretion." Good, Caitlin, I told myself. You've just made yourself sound like the master's faithful hound. Will you never say anything right to this woman?

"I'll tell the others a little about you before you come. Then you can introduce yourself and, well —"

"Improvise? Ad lib? Wing it?"

She smiled. "Yes."

"No problem," I assured her confidently.

She looked appraisingly at the street. "The light's green, and the rain seems to be letting up. I think I'll make a dash for it. Until tonight?"

"Until tonight."

Chapter 4

I pulled into my driveway at the same time Malcolm and Yvonne were pedaling up on their bicycles. They waved, and wheeled the bikes up onto the back porch. Looking like overgrown children in their yellow rain slickers, they poked their heads around the corner of the house.

"Coming up for tea?" Yvonne inquired.

"Well," I equivocated, slamming the door of my car and standing indecisively in the drizzle. I did want to talk to them, but tea with Malcolm and Yvonne was such an insufferably healthful event.

"Thanks, yes," I called. "I'll be up in a few minutes. Have to feed the cat first."

Inside, I shed my damp windbreaker, toweled my hair dry, and toted my gun into the bedroom closet.

"Repo?" I called as I put my gun away in its shoebox.

As I expected, there was no reply.

"What is this — a battle of wills?" I called to the Stygian depths. "If it is, then I give up. You win, kiddo. Just tell me what it is you *want* — different food, a new scratching post, fresh catnip. Just tell me! A feline mind reader I'm not."

Immediately, I felt guilty. Who but a low, scurvy swine would badger a sick cat? I thought of my plans to take Repo to the vet and ground my teeth. The day was good as done. The trip would have to be postponed until tomorrow. But what if Repo really *was* sick? This was the old familiar refrain — too much to do and too little time to do it in.

I changed the water in Repo's bedroom dish and went on into the kitchen to fortify myself with a snack before enduring Yvonne's tea. In the fridge I found the tail-end of some rye bread and a few pieces of lean roast beef. I spread the bread liberally with horseradish and mustard, then munched thoughtfully, staring out the kitchen window.

Autumn. Soon to be winter. Another year gone. What had I accomplished, I asked myself. Had I done anything to be proud of? Anything that mattered? For the life of me, I couldn't think of a single thing.

I remembered that when I was a little girl, I used to rush in from school, bursting to tell my grandmother what I had learned that day. We'd pour over maps of Europe, drawings of flowers, the rise

49

and fall of kings. She always made me feel that I had done something worthwhile. I realized bleakly that these days I had no one to whom I could rush home and recount my exploits, even if I'd wanted to. And besides, what exploits could I legitimately brag about?

Then, in that moment, I had the panicky feeling one gets in dreams, of being drawn inexorably toward the brink of some chasm. So real was the feeling that I clutched the table behind me for support. But in another moment the feeling was gone and I was myself again, safe in my own kitchen, in control of my life. What's going on, I wondered in alarm. Was I coming unglued? I snorted, rejecting the possibility. Probably just low blood sugar. Or PMS.

Brushing the rye bread crumbs off my turtleneck, I went upstairs for tea.

* * * * *

"Ninth Life?" Malcolm said, his periwinkle-blue eyes gazing off into the middle distance. "I think I've heard something about it, but I can't remember what." Rolling up the sleeves of his red flannel shirt, blond brows knit in thought, he returned to slicing a dark, fruity-looking cake.

"I think I remember," Yvonne said, teakettle in hand. She poured boiling water into the teapot, then pulled off her apron. Like Malcolm, she was sturdy, blonde, and blue-eyed. Her hair was earlobe-length and silky-looking, bangs cut straight across her forehead in an old-fashioned pageboy. Her eyes, as impossibly blue as Malcolm's, regarded me thoughtfully. "They're a rather, well, *secret* animal

50

rights organization. Each member only knows a few others. Sort of like a communist cell."

I raised an eyebrow. "Tut. Such melodrama."

Malcolm shook his head, bringing a plate of fruitcake slices to the table where I sat. "Not really. Those animal rights activists are always in hot water with the law. And some of them are wanted on so many charges that they daren't show their faces in public."

I thought of Judith's reluctance to meet in a public place. Maybe she wasn't so crazy after all. "What kinds of charges?"

"Oh, theft of government property, for one," Malcolm said.

"That means they broke into a government-funded lab somewhere and rescued the animals who were being tortured," Yvonne said heatedly. "Like the cats who were being used in those awful head injury experiments for example. They're still missing, and the so-called thieves are now considered national security risks." She put her hands on her hips, her eyes blazing blue fire.

"Trespass, breaking and entering, grand theft," Malcolm continued. "Those are the usual charges. Most of the activists are wanted on dozens of warrants. The police would love to get their hands on them." He served me a slice of cake and regarded the plate thoughtfully. "And the saddest part of all this is that the more successful the animal activists get — rescuing animals from some perfectly awful experiments — the less effective they can be. It's a real Catch-22 situation."

"Why? I don't understand."

His smile was even sadder. "Because none of the guerrillas — the front-line activists — dare testify in court. Don't you see? They're the ones who have firsthand knowledge of what's going on in the labs because they saw it. But they can't go into court with their evidence because they'd be admitting to crimes much more serious than those they're accusing the researchers of." He shook his head.

Yvonne put the teapot on the table and sat down. "The animal rights people say our society values almost anything else more highly than it does the lives of animals," she said. "They accuse us of being speciesists, of acting as though only human life counts upon this spinning mud ball. Sometimes I think they're right. After all, if a few dozen cats or rabbits die in an experiment designed to perfect a new football helmet, well heavens, hasn't it all been worthwhile?"

Malcolm poured tea, and I sipped slowly, for once uncritical of the healthful concoction. I was disturbed by what my two friends were telling me.

"To get back to your question about Ninth Life," Malcolm said, "I seem to recall that their big thing was to remain 'clean.' They want their group to be above reproach so they can take the evidence into court without worrying about the bailiff's heavy hand descending on their shoulders."

"I see," I replied, a little uneasy about my new assignment.

"What's your interest in all this?" Yvonne asked.

"I, um, met someone recently who's involved in this line of work," I said vaguely. "I just wanted some background."

"We have lots at the store," Malcolm said. "Brochures, pamphlets, paperback books, and so on. We have a clipping file, too, and some addresses of organizations you can write to for more information."

"Thanks," I said. "I might come around and look through your stuff." I finished my cake. "Say, what was this?" I asked. "It was delicious."

"Persimmon bread," Yvonne said, her eyes twinkling. "Some friends brought us a whole basketful of fruit. And the bread doesn't have a speck of sugar in it."

Persimmons? I thought fast, finally concluding that I had never even seen a picture of a persimmon let alone beheld one in the flesh, so to speak. "What the heck," I said magnanimously. "it was good, anyhow."

"Want the recipe?" Yvonne teased.

"No thanks," I said, playing the game. "I've done my baking for the week." Ye gods, if the bread had persimmons in it, there was no telling what desiccated exotica the tea might have contained. I decided not to ask. "Gotta run," I said, taking my plate and mug to the sink.

Yvonne walked me to the door. "Try to get more sleep," she said, hugging me. "You're looking a little under the weather."

"It's my Celtic blood," I said. "We always look pale and wan. We're delicate creatures — poets, bards, soothsayers. You great blond louts, on the other hand, always look healthy. It's your barbaric Norse ancestry. All that swinging of broadswords and battle axes and swilling of mead. It's in your genes now."

"Out!" she said, laughing, "or I'll send some persimmon bread home with you." Her expression became serious. "Are you sure —"

"Aargh," I said in mock horror. "Enough health food, woman. Say goodnight to your Viking mate for me. I'll think of you as I'm trying to resist some cholesterol-filled snack."

"You're hopeless," she told me as I hurried off down the stairs.

"True," I muttered to myself. "But therein lies my charm."

* * * * *

The Ninth Lifers' house was easy to find, just as Alison had promised. A large brown two-story structure, it sat foursquare on its lot, curtained front windows peering blankly at the sea. There were already three cars in the driveway, so I found a parking place on the street and shut off my headlights. It was just before seven, and already fully dark.

My knock was answered at once, and I was irrationally pleased to see Alison at the door. She wore the same fisherman sweater and navy pants, and her cheeks had a healthy pink glow. I smiled at her a little more fatuously than I meant to.

"C'mon in," she said. "There's a fire in the living room. Go on in and get warm. The others are out back getting wood or some such thing. Oh, would you like some coffee?"

"Yes, thanks. Black."

I wandered into the living room. Two rust-colored

tweed sofas and a pair of beige easy chairs formed three sides of a square — the fireplace formed the fourth. In the center of the room sat an immense coffee table whose base seemed to be a trio of tree trunks and whose top was an etched brass plate at least six feet in diameter. It was loaded with magazines, newspapers, yellow lined legal pads, pens and pencils. Bookcases lined the walls, and they were stuffed with stacks and stacks of manila and accordion folders. Piles of photos covered a table against the wall. This was clearly a room in which work was done. Ninth Life was, if nothing else, industrious.

"Coffee," Alison said, coming up behind me. I turned and took the mug she held out. "You'll see once we get started that this is a council of war tonight. A few of us are a little impatient with the speed we're moving at against Living World. The dissenters have some ideas of their own, they say." She frowned. "I wonder what's keeping them outside?"

As if on cue, the back door slammed, and two people entered, one carrying wood. A tall, rangy, red-haired woman glared briefly at me, then crossed her arms and leaned against the wall. Disagreeable Voice, aka Judith Hadley, I was willing to bet. The wood bearer was a young man of about thirty, with pale skin, intelligent brown eyes, and a shock of dark hair that fell over his forehead.

"Judith Hadley, Ian Burns, this is Caitlin Reece."

"Pleased to meet you," Ian said politely, depositing his wood on the hearth, dusting his hands off on his corduroy pants and brushing the hair out of his eyes. He tucked the tail of a blue wool shirt into his pants. "Liz is just doing something at her car. She'll be here in a minute."

Hands in pockets, Judith leaned against the wall, staring daggers at me and saying nothing.

"Oh, come off it, Judith," Ian said, flinging himself down into one of the chairs. "What happened to Mary certainly wasn't Caitlin's fault. We all knew that she was in trouble at Living World. That she was going to ask Caitlin for help."

"We should never have agreed to that," Judith said, acid in her voice. "It was a dumb plan. She should have been able to come to us if she was in trouble."

"She told us why she preferred to involve Caitlin," Ian said reasonably. "She didn't want to lead them to us. You heard her phone message."

"The phone message be damned," Judith said, venom in her eyes. "All I know is that this *detective* is the last person she contacted. And now she's dead."

We traded stares and I rose to my feet. If we were going to insult each other, I wanted to do so at eye level.

Misinterpreting my action, Alison stepped between us. "No, please," she said to me, laying a restraining hand on my arm. "Judith's just upset." Clasping her hands together, she looked over at Judith. "Judith," she pleaded, "you said there'd be none of this. Caitlin's agreed to help us."

Personally, I felt like smacking the truculent Judith in the chops. But presumably Alison knew better than I how to deal with her.

"Oh?" Judith asked. "Like she helped Mary? Then where are the photos? And where's the cat?"

I tossed the envelope containing the photos down on the coffee table. "The photos are here, for what they're worth," I said. "As for the cat, he's lucky to be alive." I told them what I had learned from Gray just before I left my house. "He has a raging infection in both eyes and temperature of a hundred and eight. He's receiving proper care, but he may not live through the night. And if he does, he'll almost certainly be blind."

"Damn it!" Judith said, blue eyes blazing. "He was our best piece of evidence so far."

Ian, Alison, and I all looked at each other. "A little more compassion wouldn't hurt, Judith," Ian told her. "Think of what the animal's been through."

Judith made a dismissing motion with one hand. "I've always thought you were too tender-hearted for this, Ian," she told him. "If we waited for people like you to get us results, we'd wait forever." Breathing heavily, she turned her Gorgon-like gaze on me. "And you, what about you, Caitlin Reece? Do you have any guts?"

Out of the corner of my eye I saw Ian shake his head. Presumably they played these little parlor games often.

"Oh, I have guts," I told her quietly. "But I have brains, too. I usually try using them first."

"Hmmph," she said, clearly at a loss for words.

"Then you'd better use them fast," a voice said from behind me. I turned. A small, dark-haired woman came into the room, tossing her parka over the back of a chair.

57

"Liz," Alison said. "This is —"

"I can guess who this is," the woman said, eyeing me.

I was getting a little tired of being the object of these folks' displeasure. Heck, they didn't even know me.

"The great detective." She took two steps toward me and fingered my suede windbreaker. "Nice," she commented. "Lambskin by the feel of it. An animal had to die for your vanity." She skewered me with an accusing look. When I said nothing, she turned to the others. "How can we trust anyone who supports the industries that slaughter animals for their hides?"

"Oh, Liz," Alison said in evident dismay.

"Oh, Liz," Liz mocked her. "I'm right and you know it." She turned on me again. "Why exactly are you here?"

"Because Alison asked her to help," Ian said, rising to his feet.

Oh goody, I thought, now we're all upright. We'll be swinging on each other any minute now.

Liz grinned, a sly, secretive smile. "Well, she has four days to work a miracle."

"Four days," Alison exclaimed. "What do you mean?"

"We've formed a new organization," Judith explained, looking at Alison rather apologetically, I thought. "And on Saturday — which is, as we all know, International Day of Shame for animals used in cosmetic and household products testing — we intend to put an end to Living World's operation."

"A new organization? What on earth are you talking about?" Alison asked. "We already have an organization. What —"

"No," Liz said, interrupting her. "*You* have an organization. There's no place for people like Judith and me in Ninth Life. You want to sit around and plan strategy. We want to *act*. My God, Alison, the very creatures you want to help are dying in droves while you plan — what? The best media approach?"

"You want to be guerrillas," Ian accused them. "I might have guessed it. Dammit, Liz, I thought we settled this issue when you joined us in Alberta. Of course we want to use the media. We need good press to influence public opinion. You know as well as I do that if we go around smashing and burning, we'll only antagonize people." He flung the wing of hair out of his eyes. "For God's sake, be sensible."

Judith shook her head. "We're through being sensible. We've worked for seven months here in Victoria to get the goods on Living World and where has it gotten us? Nowhere." She cracked her knuckles one by one, and I got the distinct impression that she'd rather be cracking skulls. "Well, we have a better idea. And it hasn't taken us seven months to come up with it, either. Show them, Liz."

Liz reached into the back pocket of her jeans and tossed a pamphlet at me. Reflexively, I grabbed it. It was printed on glossy white stock, and on the front a stylized claw was depicted ripping a sheet of paper. Through the tears in the paper could be seen a photo of a laboratory, with hundreds of rabbits held in restraints.

THESE RABBITS ARE DYING
FOR YOUR NEXT DATE

read the caption at the bottom.

I opened the brochure. In a very few words — and two large photos of researchers putting paste into rabbits' eyes — the text explained how thousands of animals died each year so that new cosmetics — shampoo, soap, make-up, lipstick, eyeliner — could be brought to the market. I turned the brochure over. On the back was a figure dressed in a ski mask and dark clothes, a rabbit held protectively in one arm, the other black-gloved hand raised as if to fend off a blow. "Help them fight back!" the caption exhorted. "Support us. We're Citizens for the Liberation and Welfare of Animals." Beneath the final bit of text was the same stylized claw that had appeared on the front of the brochure, and a post office box to send donations. I knew that the brochure had been designed to appeal to my emotions, to jerk me around, but dammit, it worked. I felt what anyone would feel when reading it — disgust, pity, outrage, and guilt.

"Oh, Judith," Alison said wearily, sitting down. "This is exactly what we had agreed we wouldn't do."

"No," Judith said, looking at Alison. "It's what *you* agreed we wouldn't do."

I looked from one to the other of them, realizing at last this disagreement wasn't really about Ninth Life at all. It was about power. It was also about Judith and Alison. Or maybe Judith and Mary and Alison. I looked over at Liz where she now stood, leaning against the doorframe, hands jammed in the pockets of her jeans, brown eyes on Judith, and thought I understood. I was willing to bet that it was Liz, not Judith, who had been the moving force behind CLAW, or CLAWA, or whatever it was.

Judith, Alison, and Ninth Life — so Alison had intimated — went back a long way. And while the two had not been entirely in agreement on every issue, Alison had hinted, they had agreed to disagree. I imagined Judith had restrained her hot-headedness in favor of Alison's good sense. It seemed like a workable partnership to me. So what had happened? Mary, I guessed. Once there had been Judith and Alison; then there was Judith, Alison, and Mary; and now there was Judith and Liz. I groaned. Change lobsters and dance. Well, causes loftier than Ninth Life's had been derailed by the stirrings of the libido. Unfortunate though, how much havoc can be wreaked before the itch is finally scratched.

"C'mon, Judith," Liz said peremptorily, eyeing the rest of us spineless worms in obvious disgust. "The pamphlets are loaded in my car. Let's go."

Judith took one last, eloquent, baffled look at Alison and turned to go.

"Liz, you can't be serious about giving us until Saturday," Alison said. "It's not reasonable."

"Oh, we're dead serious," Liz replied. "If Living World isn't closed down by the weekend, we'll close it down. End of discussion." She sneered a little, clearly enjoying her position of superiority over Alison.

There's nothing like being able to call the shots to bring out the best in people. I raised my eyebrows, wondering how long this particular confrontation had been brewing.

"Who'll do the dirty work?" Ian asked, sounding tired. "The two of you? As I recall, you were always full of talk, Judith, but when it came to the crunch you let Mary go undercover at Living World. You didn't offer to go."

61

"That's enough," Judith whispered, white around the lips.

"We don't need to listen to this," Liz said, hurrying over to put an arm around Judith. "And for your information, you gutless little turd," she told Ian, lip lifted in scorn, "CLAW has dozens of active members. And hundreds of supporters. We have both the muscle and the will to do what needs to be done."

Ah, but do you have the brains, I wondered. I decided it would be the wisest course of action to keep my mouth shut. One usually learns more that way. Besides, it's often dangerous to attempt to mediate internecine strife.

With a last enigmatic look at Alison, Judith allowed herself to be led away. Alison covered her face as the back door slammed, and Ian seemed too discouraged even to push the hair out of his eyes.

"Damn it," he said finally as a car engine started. "I'm going out to the Dog and Pony and get drunk. Are either of you interested?"

"Not right now," Alison said, wiping her eyes.

"No thanks," I told him, only half my mind on what he was saying.

He shrugged and walked dispiritedly into the hall. I heard the sound of a jacket being zipped, the front door opening and closing, and finally, a motorcycle being coaxed into life.

"I feel so . . . helpless," Alison told me as Ian drove off. "It's the end of Ninth Life."

"Not necessarily," I said, coming over to sit on the hearth beside her chair.

She laughed a little — a choked, unhappy sound. "How can it not be? Liz and Judith will do

62

something perfectly awful on Saturday. Dammit, they'll destroy all the careful preparation we've made, all the sympathy we've aroused, all the work we've done." She clenched her fists and struck the arm of her chair angrily.

Atta girl, I thought. Get mad. "They won't if we beat them to it," I told her.

She looked at me in evident amazement, gray eyes wide. "If we —"

"Yup."

"But how on earth can we — can you — do in four days what we've been unable to do in all these months?"

I shrugged. "Urgency sometimes leads to creative solutions."

She began to laugh in earnest this time. "Is that a quotation?" she asked. "It sounds so bloody pompous. Like something Margaret Thatcher would say." She dissolved into laughter again.

I grinned a little in agreement. I hadn't meant it to sound pompous, but she was right. Well, there were worse people to sound like than Margaret Thatcher. And I was glad I had made Alison laugh.

"You're serious, aren't you?" Her fit of laughter had subsided.

"Yes."

"I don't know," she said, shaking her head. "I appreciate your optimism, but how realistic is it? We've been trying —"

"For months," I said. "I know. Seven of them. Well, what do we have to lose by trying for four days longer? And if, as you say, the credibility of this organization is at stake, then maybe we should try pretty bloody hard. Ninth Life isn't dead yet. Maybe what we should be holding here is a pep rally instead of a wake."

She blinked. "You really *are* serious."

"That's what I'm paid for," I told her.

"All right," she said at last. "I'll need to fill you in on some background. Things that might help. I hope you've got a while."

I smiled encouragingly. "I've got all night."

Chapter 5

Four hours later, I found a parking place across the street from the Dog and Pony. I stood indecisively beside my car for a moment, a cold wind from the sea ruffling my hair. My brain felt stuffed to bursting with what Alison had told me, and I took in a lungful of cold sea air, trying to clear my mind. The bar's door opened, disgorging a handful of late-night patrons onto the sidewalk, and they staggered down Foul Bay Road, laughing uproariously and slapping each other on the backs.

I hate places like the Dog and Pony. They're

small, dark, smelly, and filled with people who don't want to go home. If I'm going to drink, I want to enjoy a few beers with my friends, out in the sunshine after an afternoon of volleyball, not in the company of strangers, crouched in the dark as though we're all engaged in some shameful ritual. The myth of the friendly neighborhood bar is just that — a myth. I've seen too many paychecks and too many relationships founder on the rocks of the local watering hole. I zipped my collar a little higher and went in search of Ian.

Inside the pub, the air was so thick with smoke you could chew it. I coughed a little, remembering another reason why I disliked these places so much. As I looked around for Ian, two burly, bearded fellows at the bar looked me over with an interest I began to find annoying. One of them elbowed the other, then heaved himself off his bar stool and ambled toward me.

"Want a little company, honey?" he asked, breathing beerily into my face.

"No," I answered firmly, finally locating Ian at a table in the far corner. I turned my back on the bearded beer drinker in preparation for threading my way through the crowd, when suddenly I felt fingers clamp closed around my left arm just above the elbow. I groaned, knowing exactly what was coming next. Men never learn. Beer Drinker pulled me around to face him, and I let him do it. I needed to be close to do what I was going to do. Good and close.

"You oughta be nicer," he said blearily. We were almost the same height, I noted. Now that I was nice and close I noted, too, the dirty jeans and the flannel shirt that smelled of old sweat.

"Let go of my arm," I said quietly.

He bared his teeth in what was most definitely not a smile. As his hand on my elbow rubbed up and down against my left breast, he arranged his mouth in a leer. I knew precisely what he was thinking — a series of contemptuous adjectives preceding the word "female." Boy, was he going to show me what I was going to get for daring to come into this he-man's domain alone, unescorted, in the middle of the *night* for God's sake. And daring to spurn his advances. Why, I deserved everything that was coming to me. And he and his buddy were going to march me outside and see that I got it. The noise was so loud, and the crowd so thick in the Dog and Pony, that I doubted anyone would have paid attention if I had screamed my head off. Which I had no intention of doing.

"C'mon now," he said, tugging my arm. "We'll just take a little walk."

So I did. I planted my left leg, swiveled the right side of my body into his, reached down with my right hand, and clamped my hand firmly around his balls. His look of bewilderment changed instantly to shock, then to pop-eyed agony as I squeezed. And squeezed . . . and thanked an Irishman named Brendan for my strong right hand. Years ago, Brendan, my firearms instructor, a taciturn ex-IRA type, had made me feel like a wimp for having weak hands. While the class looked on, he had me dry-fire my .357 as many times as I could in sixty seconds. I didn't know at the time that this was every firearms instructor's standard humiliation for novices — I just knew that I felt like a sissy. At thirty seconds I thought my finger would fall off. At forty-five seconds I had to mutter nonsense verse to make myself go on. And when sixty seconds had finally passed, I couldn't let go of the gun because my finger had cramped so badly it was fastened like a claw around the trigger.

"Forty-two," Brendan had said in disgust. "Reece, you're going to have to do better than that. A hell of a lot better. We need to make your hand as strong as a vise. A vise, hear! Because you're going to use it for things you never dreamed of."

"Yessir," I had mumbled, trying to pry my finger off the trigger. I never forgot that lesson, nor the other skills I had learned in Brendan's class. I thought about him as I squeezed this lout's balls, and silently thanked Brendan for teaching me things I had never dreamed of. Squeezing a little harder, I backed Beer Drinker up to his bar stool.

"I'm going to let go now," I said sweetly. "And you're going to sit down and be a good boy, or take your jacket and leave. I don't much care which." I let go and stepped away from him, flexing my fingers, smiling an innocent girlish smile. Beer Drinker had evidently decided not to sit down. Instead, he collapsed against his friend. I could understand that he might not want to straddle the bar stool or anything else for a few days.

"You bitch," he moaned.

"Tut, tut," I said. "And only a moment ago you were upbraiding *me* for not being nice." I turned to go, and this time my progress through the crowd was unimpeded.

I found Ian sitting at a small table, nursing a pint of dark beer and looking doleful. He looked up as I approached, and I guessed from the redness of his eyes that the beer in front of him wasn't his first. He smiled a little crookedly and waved.

"The detective lady. Sit down, sit down," he said expansively. "What will you have?"

A tallish waitress in black pants and white shirt, cuffs rolled up over her elbows, towel tucked into her belt, appeared at my elbow. Her light brown hair was cut short on the top and sides, but curled irrepressibly down to her collar in back. She had jet black eyebrows and dark, dark eyes — unusual for a near-blonde, and very attractive, I thought. "Soda water, please," I told her.

She put her hands on her hips and looked at me skeptically. "Are you trying to be smart?"

I held up my hands in mock surrender. "Honest, ma'am, I swear I'm not. I'd just like something plain and fizzy without alcohol."

"Oh," she said, mollified. "Ginger ale okay?"

"Sure," I agreed.

She took a swipe with a rag at a puddle of liquid on the table and looked at me, dark eyes speculative. "I saw what you did to that guy at the bar. The guy that came on to you."

"Oh?"

She lowered her voice. "Where did you learn how to do that?"

I smiled. "I took a course."

"Oh yeah? You a cop or something?"

"No."

"A kung-fu expert?"

"No. Just a person. Like you."

She looked at me doubtfully. "How much did the course cost?"

"About two hundred and fifty dollars," I said. "But that was three years ago. It might be more now." I looked her over. About twenty-five, she wasn't as tall as I had first thought. Maybe five-ten, I guessed, and wiry rather than muscular, with square shoulders and big hands. She had a tough, no-nonsense look about her, and I realized I was liking her more and more. "The instructor teaches firearms as well as dirty tricks," I added. "It's all included in the price."

"Hmmmm," she said again, clearly thinking hard. "Do you think I could . . . that he would . . ."

I smiled. "Maybe," I said. "Got a pen?"

She handed me a ballpoint and I scribbled my phone number down on a napkin. "Call me in a couple of days. I'll try to get him in the meantime."

"Hey, thanks," she said, smiling for the first time. Her teeth were white and even. She folded the napkin and stuck it in her shirt pocket. "I'm Perry," she said. We shook hands.

"Caitlin," I told her. Her hand *was* big. Strong, too. I bet she could have dry-fired sixty or so right on the spot. "I'll call you."

She grinned, then hurried away for my ginger ale.

"Cute," Ian remarked acerbically as Perry left. "I've been coming in here for three months, and she never told *me* her name."

"Must be my charm," I told him.

"Yeah, sure," he said, downing his beer. "She

could have told me I was the wrong sex. I would have stopped trying."

Perry brought my ginger ale and declined payment. "On the house," she said, squeezing my shoulder. Wow. What a grip!

"Drinking to the demise of Ninth Life?" I asked Ian as Perry left.

"You got it."

"What are Judith and Liz, anyhow, the Dynamic Duo?" I asked in exasperation.

He frowned. "What do you mean?"

"You and Alison are ready to lie down and die. You act as though it's a foregone conclusion that you can't do anything to deter them from their appointed course."

"Are you nuts? In four days? I'm sure you talked to Alison. We've been trying to put Living World and Evan Maleck, its asshole president, out of business for years. To no avail. The media won't have anything to do with us because we can't prove our allegations. The cat Mary rescued would have gotten us a lot of good publicity. People hate seeing companion animals abused like that."

"I'm not sure what you mean. Wasn't that just business as usual for Maleck?"

"Not exactly. You see no one — not even Living World — does the Draize Test on cats' eyes. Fortunately for cats, they're unsuitable. They yell bloody murder and their eyes tear too much. Just like ours. That's why cosmetics companies test their latest batches of goop on rabbits. No yelling, no tearing."

"But the cat," I protested. "His eyes had been

burned by something pretty caustic. And they'd been clipped open, too."

Ian sighed. "That was done by one of Maleck's lab workers. Every year on the lab director's birthday, they put a cat in with the test rabbits."

"They what?"

"Yeah," Ian said, looking away. "The lab director hates cats, so they play a little joke on him just to ring his chimes. They prep a cat with the test substance, put it in the restraints along with the rabbits, and when the director sees it, he goes bananas. They're just a bunch of fun-loving guys at Living World."

"Shit," I said faintly.

Ian nodded. "Yeah, shit. The media would have loved the story of the cat, but it's too late now. It boils down to this, Detective: we get some hard evidence, or we forget it."

"Then let's get it."

"What?" he asked derisively, pushing his hair out of his eyes. "Since when have you become an expert on all this?"

"Oh, I'm no expert," I admitted, "but I do have a couple of ideas. I'm going to need some help, though."

"What kind of help?"

"I prefer to tell you when you're sober," I told him. "What I want to know now though, is if I can count on you. Will you go home and go to bed? Or are you going to keep on swilling beer and feeling sorry for yourself?"

He propped his chin up with one fist. "I've given almost four years of my life to this organization," he said. "And we *have* done some good. We got by-laws

72

passed which prohibited animal shelters on the island from selling animals for research. And we managed to persuade the SPCA to stop using the decompression chamber to euthanize unwanted animals. We put a mink farm out of business because it violated the local health code. We were making real progress, dammit! And then Living World showed up. It's occupied our attention for way too long — we haven't been able to do anything else. But it's like Fort Knox," he said heatedly. "We couldn't find one single chink in its operation until we got Mary hired on as a lab worker. And that was only because someone at the local labor board owed us a favor."

Red-eyed, he looked up at me. "Yeah, I am feeling sorry for myself. But I'm feeling sorry for the animals we won't be able to help if we're put out of business. I don't believe for one minute that CLAW will be effective. Oh, they'll probably make a big stink and get everyone upset. But they won't make a *difference*. They're kidding themselves if they think they can close Living World down. And the ill-will they create is going to spill over onto Ninth Life. They'll neutralize us." He drew circles on the table with condensation from his beer glass. "Four days, eh? Oh, why not? Maybe you can do what we couldn't." He sat back in his chair. "But don't count on me. I'm tired, Detective. I might go home — up-island. See my folks. Right now, though," he said, "I'm going to bed."

"Can you drive?" I asked him, worried.

"Yeah. I've only had three beers." He made a face. "I hate this stuff. It makes my nose clog up and my eyes scratchy. Gives me a headache, too. But it's what people do for occasions, right?"

"Occasions?"

"Yeah, occasions. Celebrating good fortune or mourning bad fortune." He stood up and slipped his arm into his black leather motorcycle jacket. Putting his helmet under his arm, he fiddled with the zipper of the jacket. "Maybe Liz is right," he said. "Maybe I am a gutless turd. But I agree with Alison. Our cause —" he said with a lopsided, derisive smile, "animal rights — is an important one. And we're just now starting to get people on our side. We can't afford to alienate them. We have to do things *right*."

I was aware that this last message was meant for me. "I'll check with you and Alison tomorrow. Maybe you'll have changed your mind."

"Maybe," he said, looking troubled. He smiled a little. "See you." He zipped his jacket up, took a firmer grip on his motorcycle helmet, and walked off.

I swallowed the last of my ginger ale and followed him.

* * * * *

Midnight again. I stood in my kitchen, making cocoa. Well, hotshot, I asked myself, what *do* you have in mind? Pouring the hot chocolate into a mug, I added a splash of Scotch, and took it into the bathroom. While the tub was filling, I sat on the edge, thinking. Ideas careened around in my mind like gerbils in a cage. Which of them was most feasible in the short time remaining, I wasn't sure. I'd have to sleep on them.

Shedding my clothes, I slipped into the bath with a sybaritic sigh. There's nothing more conducive to right-brain activity than a cup of cocoa and a hot

74

bath. I felt myself relaxing immediately. No dawdling, now, I told myself, taking another sip of cocoa. You're in here to think, not to enjoy yourself. Where do you think you are — in a California hot tub?

The sound of my own heavy breathing — well, snoring really — woke me, and I realized that my bathwater was now distinctly cool. I fished for the plug with my toe and pulled, rationalizing that a whole lot of right-brain activity had probably gone on while I was resting my eyes. In fact, I realized, as I stood up and wrapped myself in a towel, one of the ideas that had been chasing itself around in my brain was a lot more developed than it had been an hour earlier. *See,* I told my disapproving left brain which had wanted me to sit down with a yellow tablet and make a list. *Don't be so skeptical. To paraphrase the guy touting the Paul Masson vintages, 'We will serve no idea before its time.' So there.* Yes, indeedy, I thought, toweling dry and pulling on my sweats-cum-pajamas, I liked this idea very much. It had about it a certain . . . panache. It couldn't do Ninth Life any harm, and it would certainly spell *finis* to Evan Maleck's activities. If I could pull it off. And that was a big if. I yawned hugely, heading for the bedroom. Tomorrow was soon enough to start getting my ducks in a row. After all, I had four whole days left.

TUESDAY

Chapter 6

Veterinarian Emma Neely answered my knock on her back door just before six. She ushered Repo and me into a little hall that contained rubber boots, coats and jackets on a rack on the wall, and a stack of animal carriers.

"My God, it's the prodigal daughter," she said gruffly.

I felt guilty. It was true — lately, only Repo's care brought me out to Emma's.

"I wouldn't do this for anyone but you, sweetie," she said, and I felt a little better until I realized she was talking to Repo. The prodigal daughter was evidently in the doghouse. "Take him on into the back and get started," she told her assistant, a sturdy-looking young woman with braids and freckles, blue denim shirt flapping out over her jeans. "You know what to do, Ginny."

"Does she?" I asked Emma after Ginny had left with Repo. "Your assistants look younger every year. That one can't be more than twelve."

She raised an eyebrow at me. "That sounds like the carping of a middle-aged grouch."

"Oh, all right," I admitted. Come to think of it, I was getting a trifle testy about my age. "What's she going to do to him?"

"The usual tests — blood pressure, temperature. We'll do a little blood work, and take a look at his urine. We should be able to rule out a lot of things by tonight."

"Okay," I said. "I'll stop back by later on. Sorry I can't be more precise."

Emma smiled, tucking a few loose strands of graying brown hair back behind her ears. I hadn't seen her in, oh, twelve months, and I realized with a start that she was looking every year of her fifty-five. Or was it fifty-six? Her hair was definitely more gray than brown, and her fiercely snapping dark eyes seemed to me to be just a little softer. Was it possible that she was mellowing, turning from the curmudgeon I loved into a civil-tongued dowager? What a terrible thought.

"Precise?" she snorted. "Since when were you ever precise? It isn't your strong point. As I recall, however, you do have several more interesting qualities."

80

I blushed. Emma had rented out part of her house to me when I was new to Victoria and she was practicing her profession in town. She knew me pretty well. And for her part, I was happy to see that she was as sharp-tongued as ever.

"As long as it's before midnight, just drop in," she told me. "I'll be here. And if I'm not, it's just because I've gone to the store or something. Ginny and my other assistant, Peg, live in the trailer out back. Knock and they'll let you in. They can entertain you until I get back. So long, Caitlin," she said, patting me on the cheek. "I have to go to surgery now. See you later. And don't worry. We'll find out what's wrong with Repo."

It was with a huge sense of relief that I drove away from Emma's. She *would* find out what was ailing him; I was sure of that.

* * * * *

As I drove down Saanich Highway, toward town, the sun came up — a crescent of orange-red fire, just rising over the teeth of the mainland mountains. Snowcapped Mount Baker on the American coast was briefly splashed with reflected light and it shone vividly amber, then peach and salmon, as the sun edged higher in the sky. My car topped a little hill, and I slowed down to look around. The sky was powder blue and cloudless, with a scoured-clean look to it, and the ocean off to my left was a deep, fathomless indigo. Winter colors.

I let my eyes travel to the horizon and reminded myself again why I live here — because I fell in love with the ocean and never quite got over it. I wasn't born and raised on Vancouver Island — my family lived in the Ottawa Valley for most of my life. But I remember clearly when I first came to Vancouver Island — on a business trip while I was still living in the east. I left Toronto in the middle of January, on a day so cold the snow cried out when you walked on it, and landed in Vancouver in the middle of the night. There were few jetways in those days, and when I stepped outside the plane into the open air, my nose was flooded with such a profusion of warm, moist, *living* smells that I stood there with my mouth open in amazement. I recognized cedar and pine, the smell of damp earth, and something that smelled unbelievably like roses. My God, I thought, awed — this in the middle of January? But there was something else, something tangy and unidentifiable, something indescribably exotic, like an operatic *leitmotif.*

I was horribly disappointed that the windows in the Bayshore Hotel didn't open, and I hardly slept in anticipation of the next day when I could go outside and enjoy all those smells. I remember that I finally fell asleep praying "Please, no snow." I needn't have worried. As I stood in the hotel lobby the next morning, waiting for the sun to come up, I realized with a thrill that the ocean, or a tongue of it anyhow, was right *there,* right outside the hotel. I was so excited, I didn't wait for dawn. In the gray half-light, I ran down a little path through the hotel's rose garden to the sea. And as I reached the ocean's edge, the sun came up over the towers of the city behind me, turning the waters of the bay to rippled gold. A line of poetry popped into my head:

The world is charged with the glory of God;
It shall shine out like flaming from shook foil.

And suddenly I was bawling my head off — a
bundled-up Easterner, making a fool of herself in the
gardens of Vancouver's most expensive hotel. Hardly
an auspicious beginning for a love affair.

Now, nearly twenty years later, I looked out over
the October seas to the San Juan Islands, crouched
like enormous sleeping sea beasts, and felt some of
the same awe I felt on that January day so long ago.
It had taken me a little time, and some disentangling,
to move west, but when I did, I didn't stop at
Vancouver. I went all the way to Vancouver Island —
to Victoria, and the little hamlet of Oak Bay. Roses
don't bloom here in the winter, but you can smell
cedar and pine any time you like. And that
mysterious, indescribable something, that olfactory
undercurrent my eastern nose couldn't identify two
decades ago, is something I now take for granted. The
smell of the sea.

My stomach growled, bringing me back to the
present, and I took the Quadra Street exit off the
highway into town. There's a restaurant at Cedar Hill
Crossroads that serves especially good blueberry
pancakes accompanied by fat, gorgeous slices of
peameal bacon, and I had a hankering for pancakes.
Besides, I wanted to use a phone. If I was going to
be able to pull off what I had in mind for Ninth Life,
I needed help. I intended to begin asking for it now.

* * * * *

There were a couple of calls that needed to be made right away, so I ordered my breakfast and headed for the telephone. Val answered on the fourth ring.

"Hi there," I said. "It's Caitlin."

"Hi there, yourself," she answered cheerily. "Before you tell me what you want, when are we going to get together?"

An image of Val came into my mind — moss-green eyes, expensively cut reddish-brown hair, wonderful television presence. She had that sort of polished, just-right look about her that only the very rich, the very beautiful, or the very successful have. In Val's case, she was a little bit of all three. Her wealth she owed to her late politician husband — the murderous Baxter Buchanan who had cost me a few pints of blood and some broken ribs. Probably no one mourned Buchanan's demise except his tailor and his tax attorney. Val's good looks she owed to her genes and a healthy lifestyle. Her success was all her own.

"How about today?" I said, in answer to her question. "I know it's rather sudden, but it's kind of important. I need to pick your brain. And — I cannot tell a lie — I have a favor to ask you."

"Ah," she said portentously. "Well, let me look at my calendar. Hmmm, this morning is out. This afternoon, too. But how about noon? I work out then. I could meet you here at my apartment and you could talk to me while I exercise."

"Okay," I told her. "But I need you to do something for me in the meantime. Is Lorraine Shaver still your assignment editor?"

"Yes, why?"

"I need her to tell a lie for me. And even though *she* owes me a favor, too, this is something you have to know about. In case it boomerangs."

"What is it?"

"I need to get inside the Saanich branch of a mainland cosmetics firm called Living World, and I want Lorraine to call up and use Channel 22's muscle to make an appointment for one of your reporters. Me. For an interview with the director."

"Oho," she said. "But won't you need a camera crew?"

"I'll take my own." I said. "A friend."

"Who no doubt owes you a favor too," she said, laughing. "Okay. I have no problem with this. I'll tell Lorraine and she'll call you with your interview time."

"Thanks a lot, Val," I said. "Oh, and one last thing. The interview?"

"Yes?"

"It, um, has to be tomorrow. Thursday at the absolute latest."

"No promises, but we'll try our best," she said. "Anything else?"

"Not right now."

"Okay. See you at noon."

I hung up feeling hopeful. A quick check confirmed that my breakfast had not yet arrived, so I fished another twenty cents out of my pocket and dialed a number you will never find in any directory. Amazingly, Francis answered.

"This must be a mistake," I said. "I was prepared to leave a message with that infernal machine of yours, Francis. How come you're up?"

"I'm not *up,*" he said sulkily. "In fact, I'm on my way *down.* To bed. You have ten seconds to tell me what you need."

I tut-tutted a little. "Francis, don't be so hasty. I have five fat hundred-dollar bills just dying to meet you."

"You have?" he said suspiciously. "You really *must* be in a jam, Cat my dear, if you're offering money up front. Five hundreds, you say?"

I mentally kissed them goodbye. "Five."

"Hmmm. Well I suppose I *could* give you longer than ten seconds. Will fifteen be sufficient?"

"Francis," I intoned ominously.

"All right, all right. So what is it this time?"

"I need the dope on the Saanich branch of a cosmetics company called Living World, based on the mainland. And on its director, a guy named Evan Maleck. Apparently the company operated briefly in three other provinces — Quebec, Ontario, and Alberta."

"We're talking about at least four databases," Francis said. "Maybe six. And if I do some digging on Maleck himself — taxes, credit and criminal history, medical records and so on — it could be more. Much more. The five will hardly pay for all that. Maybe you could be a little more specific. You know — give me a hint."

"I wish I could," I told him. "What I need is something really horrible on Living World, or on Maleck. Something that would shock and alienate Living World's customer base — flower children grown up into save-the-earth types. Alternatively, I'd settle for something on Maleck himself that would result in tedious and protracted legal proceedings.

86

Something that would put him behind bars. Either one will be fine. Your choice."

"Got it," Francis said. "This *will* be fun. I have some super ideas already."

"Now, don't get carried away," I warned him. "I'll take the first piece of serious dirt you can find. Let's not hold out for quality."

He sniffed. "You have no sense of *style*," he complained. "No class. And you're always in such a rush."

"Ah, but I pay well, don't I?" I reminded him sweetly. "In cash, and in advance."

"Well . . ." he admitted.

"Come off it, you little leech, you know that's the bottom line. Your favorite piece of reading material is your bank statement. Why, you're such a tightwad that when you pull a dollar bill out of your pocket, the Queen blinks from the light."

"Oh, all *right*, have it your way," he said. "You know where to put the money, I presume."

I resisted uttering the quip that sprang to my lips. "Yeah, I know. And Francis?"

"Yes?"

"Try to move your butt a little on this one, even if it does offend your sense of style. I'll leave the five hundred at your mail drop, but if you can't get me something I can use by Friday morning, early, you're not getting another penny. I don't care how many databases you have to burgle. Got it?"

He hung up. Good, that meant he got it. I walked back to my table, feeling a little drained. Doing business with Francis the Ferret was always such a big deal. His sense of the dramatic meant that I had to bluster and threaten, and he had to demur and protest. Then, after I got really tough and insulted him, he caved in and agreed to do what I wanted. Me Tarzan, him Jane. This tedious little charade had to be acted out every time we did business, and although it had been somewhat entertaining in the beginning, it was starting to be a pain in the neck. But I guess if you were as good as Francis, you could make your clients jump through hoops. He claimed that no database anywhere was safe from him, and from what I had been able to learn, he may well be right. He had certainly never let me down.

I shuddered, wondering how someone grew up to be Francis. Had he been born a snoop with the soul of a moray eel, or had his mother dropped him on his head when he was a babe, addling his wits? Come to think of it, it was hard to imagine Francis's having had a mother. Poor thing — he probably had a complete dossier on her by the time he was six. And he was such an innocent-looking fellow — small, blond, rosy-cheeked, blue-eyed, cherubic. The boy next door. Except this boy was a piranha.

Motherly, gray-haired Dahlia, my favorite waitress, had noticed my return from the telephone, and produced my pancakes with a flourish.

"Lots of blueberries today, dear," she told me in a conspiratorial whisper. "And I got you extra thick pieces of bacon. I'll bet that coffee's cold." She shook her head, removing the offending brew. "You're as bad as my daughters," she opined, "always on the phone. You dig in, now, while I get more coffee."

I dug in, and was soon scarfing down the pancakes, wondering, as I always do, what the restaurant's secret ingredient is. My own blueberry pancakes invariably turn out as flat as flitters, with the berries in a clump, looking for all the world like landscape boulders on a suburban front yard. Clearly, I am not meant to cook, I decided, polishing off the bacon and thinking about ordering more. Dahlia brought the coffee, and I looked out at the sunny October sky, feeling optimistic. Two phone calls down, two to go. I finished my coffee, and fished a couple dollars out of my pocket as a tip for Dahlia. Working as a waitress was a tough job. I know. I put myself through a couple of years of college waiting on tables. I just hoped Dahlia's daughters — the ones who talked on the phone all the time — appreciated their mom's efforts.

* * * * *

"Hey, Lester," I said breezily when he answered. "What are you doing tomorrow?"

"Well, the usual," he said, sounding uncertain. "You know. Class. The paper. Then the camera shop."

"Would you consider calling in sick?"

"Well, I suppose I could," he said. "Do you, um, you know, need me?"

"Yes, Lester, I need you."

"No problem," he said, suddenly coming to life. No doubt he thought some glamorous adventure beckoned. Well it did, sort of. "Just tell me when and where."

"Down, boy. The where I know, but I'm not sure about the when. You might have to be sick Thursday and Friday, too. I thought I should warn you."

"I can handle that," he said, obviously thinking out loud. "Trevor can put the paper to bed, and

Alisha can handle things at the camera shop. Yup, I can do it."

"Okay," I told him. "Here's what I need. Get your hands on a video camera and some tape. We need to look professional — we're going to be impersonating a television camera crew. Get whatever you need to make a good showing — you know, lights, mikes, cables, that sort of thing. We're going to do an interview. Maybe have a tour."

"Indoors or out?"

"Indoors."

"Okay. I can probably have the stuff by this afternoon."

"Great, Lester. I'll call you tonight and tell you if we're on for tomorrow. It might be wise for your flu bug to make an appearance this evening."

"Gosh, I think I feel it already," he said. "I'll mention how rotten I feel at the paper. Maybe swoon a little at the camera shop."

"I knew I could rely on you. Talk to you tonight."

One last call. Boy, the phone company was making money on me today. I let Alison's number ring eleven times before I gave up. What was she doing? I wondered. Sleeping? Walking on the beach? Sitting in that big house alone, brooding? Was she still blaming herself for the disintegration of Ninth Life? And for Mary's death? I leaned against the wall and stared out into the restaurant, realizing how little I knew about Alison. And how much I wanted to know. Giving myself a mental shake, I headed for my car.

* * * * *

Back at my house on Monterey, I parked, and was absent-mindedly inserting my key in the lock when I noticed a small, folded piece of white paper tucked behind the door knocker. It read:

Hi, Caitlin. I was out walking and thought I'd drop by. Sorry to have missed you. Call me later? I'll be at home.

Alison

Irrationally, I felt that the day had become even brighter. Whistling, I went inside and locked the door behind me.

In my study, I found what I needed — a yellow legal tablet and several Bic ballpoints. Tossing paper and pens into a plastic portfolio case that my insurance agent had given me for Christmas one year when I was still a real, solvent person, I carried everything out to the kitchen table.

Maybe I wouldn't make more coffee, I decided. Malcolm and Yvonne usually had some exotic coffee brewing at the cafe, and they knew it was useless to urge tea on me once I'd gotten a whiff of Jamaican Blue Mountain or Columbian Dark Roast. I briefly considered walking to the cafe, then remembered how quickly the weather had changed the other day. No, even though it was only a dozen blocks, I'd better drive. Besides, I wouldn't want to exhaust myself. After all, there was serious detecting to be done.

Chapter 7

I headed for the back of Malcolm and Yvonne's
health food store, to the little cafe they had added
when they remodeled. Yvonne was busy at the
counter, making a smoothie for an intense-looking
young man in a long white tunic and pants. I waved
and helped myself to coffee. Kenyan, the sign by the
coffee pot said. Yummy.

I claimed the little table by the back window,
depositing my portfolio case and windbreaker on it,

and as I waited for Yvonne to finish, I ambled over to read the bulletin board.

The west coast is a hotbed of New Age spirituality, and sometimes I think all the New Agers on the continent have passed through Victoria. They don't stay here — instead, they flock to Orcas, in the San Juans. Orcas always has been a little off-the-wall — some of the residents believe that an angel who lives on top of Mount Constitution maintains the island's therapeutic atmosphere. Louis Gittner, a local psychic and hotel owner, claims that Orcas is part of the lost continent of Lemuria, a place where human souls rest while awaiting reincarnation. No wonder the New Agers feel right at home there. But nowadays the ordinary folk on Orcas are getting a little irate at the influx of dreamy-eyed souls from the mainland and the services they offer — channeling, breathing awareness, group midwifery. In the fall, a women's peace group held a weekend-long vigil to bless a 33-acre peninsula on which condominiums are to be built, and, purportedly, communed rather noisily with the property's past and future souls. That was the last straw for many longtime Orcasians. New Age is in disrepute on Orcas right now.

But judging by the number of fliers and business cards on the bulletin board, the movement itself was alive and well. Advertised were crystal channelers, aura cleansers, rebirthers, and energy balancers. There was even a flier asking for donations for a newsletter about living in trees. Clearly I was missing something. Should I try to get in touch with my past lives? Maybe Ray Kroc would be my channeler. Or Annie

Oakley. Or the goddess Diana. Perhaps I was one of the daughters of Artemis. Or maybe I should have my aura cleansed, instead. Couldn't hurt, I decided.

"Don't say a word," Yvonne warned, coming up behind me as I read.

"No ma'am," I assured her. Suddenly I saw something I recognized — a brochure with a stylized claw on the front. Tacked to it was a piece of paper advertising a meeting of the CLAW Action Committee. Tonight. I grabbed my yellow tablet and scribbled down the time and place. Action, eh? That sounded right up my alley.

"I can't believe you found something to interest you there," Yvonne said.

"Well, yes, I did sort of," I admitted.

"You must be becoming more tolerant," she speculated, raising one blonde eyebrow.

I said nothing, not wanting to give her false hope.

"The books and clippings are over there." She pointed me in the direction of a small bookcase near the coffee maker. "They're for anyone to read, and they get quite a lot of use. People contribute to the clipping file, so it should be fairly comprehensive. Would you mind looking at the stuff here? You know, not taking it out of the cafe?"

"Not at all," I said, showing her my yellow tablet. "See — I came prepared to take notes."

She looked at me skeptically. "What's this *really* all about, Caitlin?"

"Just . . . educating myself," I said evasively. "I'll be talking to the animals one day soon, and want to be sure I know the right language to speak."

She shook her head and hurried back behind the counter to whip up some more smoothies. I looked at my watch. Nearly ten. If I didn't hurry, I'd find myself eating lunch here, courtesy of Malcolm and Yvonne. I furtively studied the chalkboard, noting with sinking heart that the lunch choices were Leek and Brown Rice Soup, and Four Mushroom Casserole. Swell. I was willing to bet that the mushrooms had come in a cellophane bag with arcane Oriental script, and looked like dried boxers' ears. No way was I eating here today, free lunch or not. I walked over to the bookcase and stood there for a moment looking at titles, hands in my pockets.

"Planning on doing some reading?" a disagreeable-sounding voice inquired from behind me. I groaned. Judith.

"It's never too late to learn," I told her with false heartiness. "Don't educators tell us that learning's a lifelong process?" I turned to face her.

She looked terrible this morning — pale and wan, her red hair lank and greasy. She was dressed in exactly what she had been wearing the night before and it, too, looked a little the worse for wear. I guessed Judith and Liz had had a busy night hustling brochures or plotting in a dimly lit room or whatever it was activists did. In reply to my question, Judith huffed a little and frowned.

I decided to take advantage of her weakened condition. "Let's have a truce, Judith," I proposed. "I *am* here to learn. Maybe you could help me."

She blinked several times. "Oh?" she asked suspiciously. "Just what is it that you think you want to learn?"

"About all this," I replied, gesturing to the bookcase.

She laughed — a bitter, grating sound. "No you

95

don't," she assured me. "Not really. You can say we're all fighting the good fight together, but we're not. You don't really care. Alison's paying you to care."

I said nothing. She had a point, albeit a tiny one: Alison *was* paying me. But I felt a little aggrieved, too. Heck, I liked animals as much as the next person. Who was Judith to say I didn't care?

"Well?" she prodded.

"What can I say?" I asked her. "You have me pegged as one of the bad guys."

"Well, aren't you?"

"I —"

Angry, she cut me off. "You what? You're with us in principle? Bull! I've put my butt on the line for what I believe in more times than I can count. What about you? What do you do besides take money to poke around in other people's business?"

I frowned. This was a reprise of last night. I didn't deserve such antagonism, and in a small flash of clarity, I understood something. Judith was a soul in pain, and this attack on me was her way of dispelling the hurt. She was attacking me because she could — because I was a handy and acceptable target. But who was the real target? Who had really hurt her? I decided to push her a little to try and find out.

"Listen, you're wrong about me. I care about animals as much as the next person."

That did it. A fanatical gleam came into Judith's eyes and color blossomed in her cheeks. "And you're just as ignorant as the next person," she hissed. "Willfully ignorant. You and all the other 'next persons' are like the good German burghers in World

96

War Two who denied there were death camps. You and the rest of the public don't want to know what you're really paying for when you support medical research. Well? *Do* you want to know?"

Even though I didn't, I nodded yes. Anything to keep her talking.

"Let's take all the tax dollars being poured into our number one health scourge — cancer. The Big C. Where does most of it go? Into research on animals. And why in God's name are we giving thousands and thousands of lab animals lung cancer when we already know that we could wipe out the disease if people just stopped smoking? I mean, this isn't hard to understand. This isn't Newton's Law of Universal Gravitation. This is a relationship any school kid knows — smoking causes lung cancer."

Agitated, she ran a hand through her hair. "And for that matter, how many of the results from animal models are directly applicable to humans, anyhow? We're not rabbits, or cats, or rats. Thalidomide was tested to a fare-thee-well on half the rodent population of the world, and look what good all *that* testing did."

She shook her head. "No, you and the rest of the animal lovers of the world just don't want to know certain things." She cocked her head and looked at me accusingly, and I had to admit she was right. I really didn't want to know, didn't want to hear, didn't want to see the awful pictures. Relentlessly, she continued. "If you think what's done to animals in medicine and industry is bad, then you certainly don't want to know what happens to your dinner while it's still an animal, or what the fresh-out-of-college boys in government research facilities do

97

with their lab animals. Nope, you certainly don't want to know about that, Miss Tough Detective. Well, do you?"

I cleared my throat. "If I have to." Even to *my* ears, I sounded wimpish.

She skewered me with a disgusted look. "No you don't," she said. "Because if you and all the other animal lovers had seen a fraction of what Alison and I have seen, you wouldn't be the same. No one wants to think about caustic paste being smeared in rabbits' eyes or veal calves being confined to spaces so small they can't turn around. But all you so-called animal lovers use shampoo and eat veal. You're happy to make use of these products. You simply blind yourselves to the price — another creature's suffering."

She made a disgusted sound. "Liz was right — look at that leather jacket."

By this time, I felt like an accessory to murder.

"Speciesist," she accused me.

But somehow, it was she, not I, who was distraught. To my amazement I saw her eyes brimming with unshed tears. Something was very wrong here. "Judith," I said softly, putting one hand on her arm.

She gave a choked sob, turned, and ran from the shop.

"Damn," I said, half-tempted to go after her. I had been close to something, I sensed, something that lurked behind the fireworks display. Something Judith desperately wanted to conceal. Oh, her accusations had certainly been accurate — I still smarted from some of them — but I had the feeling this was rote.

I looked back at the bookshelf and suddenly I had

no more stomach for educating myself about animal abuse. Maybe Judith was right — maybe I wasn't tough enough for all this. And as I gathered up my notepad and pen, a thought occurred to me. Judith had left one accusation unspoken. Perhaps the most important one.

If I and all the other so-called animal lovers ever acknowledged that we ought to extend to animals the same consideration we owe each other, then we would really be in trouble. Because then we'd be forced to make changes in our behavior. We'd be forced to do things differently, or live with ourselves knowing that we're hypocrites.

It was an uncomfortable thought. Because if I agreed with Ninth Life — if I *truly* agreed — then I would have to change my habits: what I ate, what I wore, what I used to shampoo my hair, brush my teeth, wash my dishes. It was a daunting proposition. And Judith was right. I wasn't up to it.

* * * * *

Feeling guilty and depressed, I escaped from the Oak Bay Natural Foods Emporium and Cafe into the bright blue afternoon. It was lunchtime and, feeling ravenous and anxious, I hurried for my car. I had intended to pick up a Big Mac on the way to meet Val, but somehow, it didn't seem appropriate. Darn it, now what? Feeling pensive, I drove through the local Golden Arches and ordered two large fries and a chocolate shake. That would just have to do until I had some time to think things over. My God, was it possible that I was about to become a vegetarian?

Horrors. I shuddered at the thought, polished off the last of the fries, and pulled into the parking lot of Val's apartment at exactly noon.

It had been my idea to sit and chat with Val as she pedaled away on the Lifecycle or bench-pressed or engaged in whatever strenuous activity she intended to pursue. Val, however, clearly had other ideas. Dressed in teal blue sweat pants and a matching hooded sweatshirt, she met me at the door of her apartment's gym/pool. After we hugged hello, she handed me a towel.

"Are we hitting the showers already?" I asked.

"Funny, Caitlin. No, we're swimming."

I thought of all those masticated fries now swimming in their very own pool of chocolate milkshake, and gulped. "Um," I said lamely, "I've just had lunch. And besides, I didn't bring my suit."

"I brought one of mine for you," she said, pointing to the towel. "We're about the same size. And we're not in training for the Olympics. It's unlikely you'll get cramps. Come on, Caitlin."

I gave in, remembering thankfully that I had shaved my legs and armpits sometime within living memory. Otherwise, Val would have been swimming with The Human Brillo Pad.

As we hung up our clothes and squirmed into the Lycra suits — mine was plain navy blue, hers was green with white racing stripes up the sides — I asked when Val had taken up swimming. Or exercise at all, for that matter.

"Oh, about six months ago," she said. "I turned forty in April. That may have had something to do with it. I can't run — my knees click so badly they sound as though I'm sending Morse code — and I'm

100

afraid to ride a bicycle. So, by process of elimination, I arrived at swimming. I just didn't want to get fat and dumpy," she told me, looking worried.

I looked her over critically. "Val, I can't see one extra pound. Fat and dumpy is not in your immediate future."

She picked up her towel and looked at me seriously. "Now that I'm . . . free, now that Baxter is dead, I've been doing some serious reevaluating of my life. I want to enjoy myself," she said matter-of-factly. "I spent a lot of years denying what I am, being ashamed of it. Hiding. There are possibilities out there. People. Experiences. When they come along, I want to be able to enjoy them."

"Oh, I get it," I told her, grinning. "You're an athlete in training for the great game of life."

"How right you are," she said, poking me playfully in the arm. "And you made it all possible. Let's go swim a little and you can tell me whatever you came here to tell me. Oh, incidentally, Lorraine got you the interview you wanted at Living World. You're lucky Maleck's going to be there. It's Wednesday at eleven — tomorrow. I hope that's okay. And I'm not going to ask what you want it for."

"Thanks for both things," I said.

We swam a little — we were the only people swimming at that hour of the day — and as we breaststroked back and forth, I told her what I wanted.

"You want me to do *what?*" she gasped, inhaling water and losing her rhythm.

So I told her again. "I'll give you some video footage. You get it aired on Friday's six o'clock news. Simple, yes?"

"Simple, no," she said. "What you're asking is, well, serious business. And complicated, too. I'd need the help of someone in the newsroom. Someone I could trust. And if anyone found out, my head would roll."

"I know," I told her. "But I wouldn't ask you if it wasn't important."

"Oh, Caitlin," she said in dismay. "Sure, I *could* do it. I could switch one of the reporters' tapes on its way to the control room. After it's been previewed and timed and so on. But it's so bloody risky. What is it, anyhow? Maybe you could give me the tape and let us make legitimate use of it. You know, give us an exclusive."

"The station couldn't use it legally," I told her. "You'd get your license pulled."

"Oh, no," she said. "You're going to break the law to get that tape, aren't you?"

"Probably," I said. She shook her head and swam away from me.

Diving underwater to make our turn, we kicked off the pool wall together. I opened my eyes to watch her, and saw her legs flash pale brown, straight and strong in the aqua half-light. Fat and dumpy, my eye. When we surfaced, I said nothing, not wanting to interrupt her train of thought.

"Okay," she said. "What you want is possible. But you have to assure me that it's for a good cause. A *damned* good cause."

"Oh, it is. It's —"

"That's enough! Don't tell me which one. When the station manager calls me in on the carpet, I want to be able to honestly say that I've never seen the tape. For the sake of the station as well as my career."

"Okay." Treading water, I asked. "Then you'll do it?" I had to be absolutely sure.

She stopped swimming, too, and we faced each other. Her green eyes were sober and serious, her dark hair plastered to her skull like an otter's pelt. She looked like a mermaid, a silkie, a water spirit. Something otherworldly, exotic, and absolutely lovely. How had I missed this when I had worked for Val last year, I asked myself, marveling. I recalled that I had been more interested in her lover, Tonia. I had had no eyes for Val. She looked at me and I knew she knew what I was thinking.

"I'll do it," she said. "I guess I'm like all those other people. I owe it to you."

"I won't ask you for another favor like this, in case you're wondering. You're off the hook."

She smiled, eyes the color of malachite, teeth white against the tail-end of a summer tan. "I don't necessarily mind being in your debt. Just as long as we both know what I can and can't deliver."

Was that a double entendre or what? I cleared my throat, feeling more than a little foolish. "Well, just be careful," I said, trying to sound stern. "This is important, but it's not worth losing your job over."

She gave me an unfathomable look. "All right."

"Let's swim," I suggested, not at all sure where I wanted this conversation to go. "Race you to the end of the pool and back."

"Okay," she said.

I won.

* * * * *

103

So far, so good, I congratulated myself, wheeling my MG out of Val's parking lot. Things were shaping up nicely. Francis was working hard at his electronic shenanigans. Val had agreed to slip a pirate tape into the middle of the six o'clock news. Fun and games. I thought I'd better tell Lester we were on for tomorrow morning. And check to see that his flu was coming along nicely. After all, I didn't want him to lose *his* job, either. I'd become fond of Lester, and I wasn't sure why. Maybe I felt guilty that he'd almost gotten killed helping me last year. Or, what the heck, maybe I just *liked* him. It was possible for a woman to just *like* a man, wasn't it? I thought so, but I wasn't sure. My radical feminist friends would probably disagree, but then they disagree with me on almost everything.

I'm not far enough along in my process, they say. Whatever that means. I can hardly believe that people I've known for years, people I went through school with, actually utter this claptrap. Give me a break! Of course Lester was about half my age. Did that fact count? Did it mean that I could like him because he wasn't a sexual threat to me? Or maybe there was another, deeper reason behind my liking. Maybe it was misplaced nurturing, like my ownership of Repo. A sort of mutated mothering instinct. I shuddered. Enough cerebration. Who knew *what* conclusions such unbridled thoughts could lead to. Ye gods — I might find that I was farther behind in my process than I realized.

* * * * *

Back at home, I phoned Lester, and was fortunate enough to get him just as he walked into the college newspaper office.

"Our interview is tomorrow," I told him. "Eleven o'clock. Did you get the camera and the other stuff?"

"Yup," he informed me in a co-conspiratorial tone. "It's all in my jeep."

"Good boy. Now what about that flu?"

"Well, thanks for the invitation," he said, hamming it up for the benefit of whoever was listening, "but I feel too rotten. I think I'm getting the flu or something."

"Nice touch, Lester," I complimented him. "I'll pick you up tomorrow at ten."

I stretched and yawned, looking out the kitchen window. The day was still bright and blue. Although the prospect of a nap was tempting, I thought I'd better turn my attention to the leaves in the side yard. Besides, all that mindless physical activity offers the right brain even more opportunities for work. And I had a feeling I was going to need all the help I could get in the next few days — from my right brain or any other source.

I went out the back door and across the yard into the little shed that I shared with Malcolm and Yvonne, hunting around for my heavy work gloves. After a few minutes of searching, I gave up. Who could find anything in the jumble of *things* I had tossed into the corner? An assortment of red clay flowerpots, bags of potting soil, miscellaneous bottles of B-1 plant food, some hand tools, a paper bag full of seed packets, and several dozen peat pots which attested to my attempts at gardening. Alas, I think I'm destined to not garden in much the same way I'm destined to not cook. Under my tender ministrations, plants immediately turn up their toes and die. Some have been known to expire on the way home from the nursery, which is, I've always thought, really quite premature of them. After all, I might have improved — read a new book, even taken a class. To tell the truth, I've read dozens of books on plants. Magazines, too. *Organic Gardening* is one of my favorite publications. But my problem is that I like to read about gardening a lot more than I like to garden. Stories of people who develop new strains of squash under grow-lights in their bathrooms, or harvest enough food to feed the entire neighborhood from an intricately watered and mulched twelve-square-inch raised-bed system make me depressed. It's not that I don't think these people and their efforts are admirable — believe me, I do. It's just that I'm not up to all the planning and preparing, the mulching and ministering, the weeding and watering. Give me strength. All that for a few dozen tomatoes? I'd rather go to Safeway.

What *does* interest me, however, and what I'll look at far into the wee hours of winter nights, are all those wonderful flower catalogs. Yup — I'm a seed catalog junkie. I got hooked on Park's and Burpee when I lived in the east. In Toronto, reading about zinnias and marigolds in the middle of January was almost a religious experience. But I never do (or did) get around to ordering anything in time to plant seeds. Then, when I start feeling a proprietary longing for my very own plot of nasturtiums, the plants never seem inclined to cooperate. Ah well. Maybe I should content myself with vicarious pleasure. After all, Victoria isn't called "Canada's best bloomin' city" for nothing. There were plenty of neighboring flower beds for me to admire. And no weeding to do.

I peered out through the shed's window at Yvonne's and Malcolm's veggie garden and shook my head in bemusement. Another of Victoria's wonders. I recognized the knee-high broccoli and cauliflower plants, but only because my tenants had taken me on a tour. The rest of what was growing in that garden was a mystery to me. In fact, several of the specimens bore a decided resemblance to the malevolent little plant in the movie *Little Shop of Horrors*. The rolls of plastic and hoops of metal stacked against the garage indicated that plans were afoot to insulate these horticultural marvels from the winter's chill. I shuddered. That was fine with me. Just as long as I didn't have to meet any of them in a casserole.

I spotted a rake on the other side of the shed, and was just about to grab it and go tackle the leaves when the phone rang. I hurried back inside.

"Caitlin," a worried voice said, "it's Alison. I went by your place earlier and left a note."

"I got it," I told her, a little surprised that she was calling. Her note hadn't suggested an emergency. Still, I was happy to hear from her. "I was going to call you tonight. What's up?"

I could hear her take a deep breath. "It's Judith. She came back to the house early this morning. We had a talk. She said she wanted me to understand that she needed to break away from Ninth Life, to join a group that will let her express feelings more directly."

"That's nothing new. She told us all about that last night. In no uncertain terms."

"I know. But Caitlin, it's what Judith *didn't* say this morning that I found disturbing."

"What do you mean?"

"Well, she didn't mention Mary. Not once. And when I did, she changed the subject."

"That's not so hard to understand."

"Oh?"

"Think about it. Isn't it logical that she resented Mary's role in Ninth Life more than she let on? The glamorous newcomer going bravely undercover — that kind of thing? You and Judith go back a long way. She probably felt, well, aggrieved. And I'm sure she entertained a number of unkind thoughts about both of you over the past few weeks. Now that Mary's dead, Judith may well be feeling guilty for what were perfectly natural reactions."

A sigh. "You make it all sound so reasonable."

"Mmmm," I replied. Reasonable? Hardly. Feelings are, by definition, never reasonable.

"Caitlin, Judith had something else on her mind. I know her too well to be mistaken. She wanted to tell me something, but couldn't."

Aha. "Do you think it was something about Mary?"

"I'm not sure. She did try once or twice to say something, and each time it was a comment of mine about Liz and CLAW that prompted it. Caitlin, I've not known her to be so inarticulate. Usually she can come right out and say what she thinks. This is clearly something difficult for her."

Interesting. "Well, there would seem to be two possibilities. Either she has something to tell you about Mary, or something to tell you about Liz and CLAW."

"Right."

"If it's sufficiently important, she'll probably try again, don't you think?"

"I hadn't considered that," Alison said, sounding more cheerful. "But now that you mention it, I think she will. You know, despite what she says, I don't think she's totally committed to CLAW. I get the feeling that despite her desire for action, there's something about CLAW that she doesn't quite like."

"Maybe it's what they're planning for Saturday," I guessed.

"Maybe so. Dammit, I wish I knew what Liz has up her sleeve."

"Maybe we can find out." I told her about the flier I had seen on Yvonne's bulletin board.

"But how can you go? They'll recognize you for sure."

"Well, I'll change my appearance a bit," I told her.

"Are you serious? A disguise?"

"Yeah," I admitted.

She laughed. "Okay. If you say it'll work."

"It'll work," I told her. "It has to. We need to know something about what they're planning and this is a meeting of the action committee."

"If they're going to survive, they can't keep advertising their meetings," Alison said thoughtfully.

"To be effective, they'll have to be more secretive. After all, they don't want outsiders to learn their plans."

How right she was. But thank heavens that in their inexperience, they'd told the world about *this* action meeting.

"They probably feel under pressure for Saturday night," she continued. "I know I would. And they're awfully new at this."

"Well, I'll see what I can find out. This is an edge we need."

"You're right." Then after a pause, she added, "Caitlin?"

"Yes?"

"Would you like to come over afterward? You could tell me what you learned."

"Sure," I said with studied nonchalance, trying my best not to sound like an over-eager fourteen-year-old. "I could do that."

"See you then," she said.

"Right," I agreed.

I sat and smiled at the phone for a full minute before I realized she had hung up.

* * * * *

Fueled by a resurgence of libidinous thoughts, I wielded my rake with enthusiasm, and in record time had the leaves piled into three humongous stacks by the garage. The phone call from Alison had, in addition to recharging my batteries, effectively reminded me that I had done nothing to earn the money she had given me to look into Mary's death. I had set the wheels in motion to help Ninth Life, but what had I done for Alison? I decided to remedy that.

I returned the rake to its resting place inside the shed and washed up. Taking a Diet Pepsi and an apple from the fridge, I sat at the kitchen table and dialed Sandy's number at the Oak Bay Police Station. After a shorter-than-usual wait, he came on the line.

"Alexander speaking."

"A slow crime day, is it?" I asked. "Why aren't you out there nabbing criminals instead of warming the seat of your office chair? My goodness, what *do* we taxpayers pay you boys for, anyhow?"

"Some of us have all the luck, I guess," he replied. "What are you up to, Caitlin Reece? I haven't heard from you in a dog's age."

"Oh well, you know," I told him evasively. "This and that. Listen, Sandy, I need a favor."

"Big or small?"

"Small. You can take care of it with a couple of phone calls."

"Shoot."

"There was an automobile accident on Sunday night. Monday morning actually. A dark red VW Bug went through the guard rail on the Pat Bay Highway. Ended up in the bay. I need to get a look at the car. And I need to know the blood alcohol count of the driver. Mary Shephard was her name."

"Letting you have a look at the car will be the easy part. The other I'll have to get from the Medical Examiner's office. That'll take time. He's a lazy swine. Monday," he muttered. "Yesterday. Hmmm. It won't be in Impound yet. Most likely it's still in Forensics' lot, awaiting someone's pleasure. Hang on and I'll call over there."

"Thanks." He put me on hold, and I slurped Pepsi and chomped my apple, waiting for him to get the information. Good old Sandy was really Detective Sergeant Gary Alexander of the Oak Bay Police Department, Major Crimes Division. A Scot, he was about fifty-five, with a sunny optimism about life I found daunting, and the most amazingly aggressive moustache I had ever seen. Sandy and I were in each other's debt for a dozen favors that dated from the time I worked in the Crown Prosecutor's office. But unlike most people, Sandy paid his debts.

"Just as I thought," he said in disgust. "It's in Forensics' parking lot out on Quadra. I'm certain Monday night's rain did the evidence a lot of good."

"Well, I'd like to take a look at it anyhow," I said.

"I thought you would," he said. "The kid on duty is a parolee. Name's Duncan. He's a disagreeable little twit, but he doesn't have any real backbone that I've ever seen." Sandy snorted. "One of the chief's rehabilitation projects. I told Forensics you're coming — you're supposed to be my mechanic. I've sent you over to kick the Bug's tires in case I decide to buy it. Duncan will try to make things difficult for you, but I'm confident you can handle it. If all else fails, you can invoke my name."

"He sounds like a swell guy," I said. "Thanks a lot, Sandy."

"Don't mention it. I'll call you with the blood alcohol count on Mary Shepard. Oh, and Caitlin?"

"Yes?"

"Be gentle with young Duncan. There's a good girl."

"I promise," I said sweetly, and hung up.

Hell's bells, couldn't anything be easy? Young Duncan sounded about as appealing as a rabid rat. Be gentle with him indeed. And I was supposed to impersonate Sandy's mechanic? Great. What I know about cars could be written on the head of an Allen wrench. You put gas and oil in them and they go. When they don't, you curse, kick them, and reach for your checkbook. Well, I guessed I could kick tires as well as anyone. Although it wasn't the Bug's tires I was interested in looking at.

In my bedroom, I hauled out a pair of voluminous gray coveralls acquired from an earlier escapade, and put them on over my jeans and turtleneck. Despite the sunshine, the day was chilly. I hunted around in the spare room and found my Polaroid camera, checked to see that it was loaded, grabbed my clipboard, and started for the front door. But halfway there, I stopped. Something was wrong. I stood in the middle of the living room for a full minute, wondering what it was before it hit me. Repo. I missed that fat furry feline so badly it hurt. There was no one to greet me when I came home, and no one to urge me to hurry back when I left. The house felt awful — lonely and empty. I realized belatedly how much a part of my life Repo had become. Dammit, I loved the portly furniture shredder. Tonight, I swore. I'll come for you tonight, guy.

* * * * *

I parked outside the chain-link fence surrounding the Forensics lot on Quadra Street, hung the Polaroid around my neck, and strode confidently up to a little hut by the gate. With a Vancouver Canucks cap on my head and my mirror sunglasses on, I was sure that I had achieved androgyny. A skinny twenty-year-old with greasy brown hair, a long, pointed nose and a terrible case of acne came out of the hut. Young Duncan, I presumed. I decided to establish who was boss here right off the bat.

"Sergeant Alexander sent me," I said authoritatively. "You Duncan?"

"Yeah," the kid said, looking me up and down appraisingly. He put his hands in the pockets of his navy coveralls and stared at me, a nasty little smile twitching his lips. I groaned. Obviously my disguise had been for naught. I would probably have gotten better results with a tight sweater and a zippered leather skirt.

"I need to see that VW Bug over there," I told him. "The red one."

"Sorry," he said, leaning against the fence. He gestured limply to the cars behind him. "All this here is evidence. I can't let civilians in here."

"Oh really?" I asked. "And Sergeant Alexander was so sure you would. As a favor to him."

"Oh yeah?"

"Yeah." I reached into the right-hand chest pocked of my coveralls and pulled out a folded twenty-dollar bill. I showed it to him. "The sergeant would be much obliged."

The kid grinned and heaved himself off the fence. He held out one grubby hand for the twenty.

"Not quite so fast," I told him. "It's not that I

114

don't trust you or anything but I can see how busy you are. In all the excitement going on around here, I sure wouldn't want you to lose track of your part of the bargain. So if it's all the same with you, I'll just hold onto the money until I'm done."

He licked his lips. "What the fuck," he said finally, fishing a key ring out of his pocket. "Have it your way." Unlocking the gate, he ushered me inside.

The Bug was parked at the end of the second row of cars, and it was a sorry sight indeed. It was obvious the driver had rolled the car — there didn't seem to be one square foot of metal that was undented. The front windshield was missing, as was one of the side windows. I recalled Sandy's remark about rain and shook my head. Well, with any luck, the evidence I wanted would still be there.

I walked around the car, looking critically. Uh huh. Just as I had hoped. On the left rear fender, driver's side, was a long, light-colored scrape. If you looked closely, you could see that it was paint. Lemon yellow paint, like the pale yellow Buick that had pursued Mary into the parking lot of the Donut Stop Sunday night. I unstrapped the Polaroid and backed up, taking an establishing shot of the car. It turned out pretty well, and I tucked it away in my pocket. Then I squatted down by the fender.

"Hey, you didn't say nuthin about no pictures," Duncan called from behind me.

Ignoring him, I took a close-up and waited for it to develop. Not bad. I decided to take another.

"Hey, lady, I'm *talking* to you!"

I sighed, got to my feet, and turned around. "What's it to you if I take pictures or just look?"

"Pictures is different," he said, displaying a set of

115

teeth that would have made a dental hygienist pale. "Pictures is, like, a whole nuther thing."

A whole nuther thing? "Oh, I get it. You mean there'll be an extra charge for pictures."

"That's what I said. And listen, I know you're not no *mechanic*. Mechanics don't take pictures," he concluded in a triumph of logic.

I had a momentary urge to plant one of my booted feet on this kid's backside and return him to his post outside the gate. Instead, I gritted my teeth and told myself to be tactful. Sandy expected it of me. "How much?"

"Well . . . let's say another twenty."

I almost laughed out loud. This kid had zero future as an extortionist. Oh, his instincts were right, but he had absolutely no idea of what the market would bear. Maybe I should introduce him to Francis, I thought. Give young Duncan a *real* role model. "Why not?" I said in a tone of capitulation. "I'll just charge the extra twenty to Sergeant Alexander." Which, of course, I had no intention of doing.

That seemed to satisfy him. As I squatted down to take another picture, he squatted down beside me. "So, like, why do you need pictures?"

I thought it best to stick to my story. "Beats me. I'm just doing a favor for the Sarge."

"Oh," he said. He ran a grubby finger over the streak of yellow paint. "Looks like it was sideswiped," he said.

"Looks that way," I agreed.

"*Are* you a mechanic?" he asked, curiosity evidently getting the better of him.

I thought this over. "Sure," I said. "I've fixed lots of things. I have quite a few satisfied customers, too."

"No shit," he said, impressed. "I didn't know they, you know, *allowed* lady mechanics."

Ah the ubiquitous "they." "Times are changing," I told him. "They're allowing ladies to do lots of things. We're mechanics, pilots, firefighters, cops — you know they even allowed a lady astronaut in space?"

He frowned, clearly trying to decide if this was fact or science fiction. "Right," he finally agreed, nodding sagely. "I think I heard about that. Say, I gotta go back to the gate. See me when you leave, okay?"

"Sure," I told him. When he was safely out of sight, I took a plastic bag and my Swiss Army knife out of my coveralls pocket. It took only a second or two to transfer some of the larger pieces of yellow paint from the Bug's fender to the plastic bag. I carefully sealed the bag, and returned it to my pocket. There. That was all I could do here. As for the yellow car that had done the sideswiping, I had the feeling I'd be seeing it very soon.

Poor young Duncan. What kind of a future did he have? Sandy had said he was a parolee. I shook my head. Prison evidently hadn't taught him any lessons — he was running his entry-fee scam here on the grounds of the police forensics lot. He was either very nervy or very stupid. Somehow, I suspected the latter. I felt sorry for him, and was glad I hadn't treated him too badly. As I walked back to the gate, I dug the extra twenty out of my pocket with scarcely a twinge of regret.

"Here you go," I told him, proffering the money.

"Thanks," he said, spiriting it away into some interior pocket.

"Take care, now," I said, motivated by a desire to say something kind.

He looked at me a little suspiciously, too dull to resent my interest in him, in the poor young Duncan dozens of others had probably tried to help. "Hey, I always take care of Number One," he said with a fatuous grin. "Always."

Chapter 8

Five o'clock found me prowling the aisles of the Oak Bay Safeway store. I had a hunger that couldn't be appeased by any number of the Golden Arches' fries, and the thought of eating meat was an issue I still hadn't resolved. So I decided to play it safe and make a visit to the frozen foods section of the supermarket. When I did so, I went into shock. Have you *seen* the variety of packaged foods for non-cooks? After a tour of the freezers, my brain was reeling. How long had this world of culinary delights been hidden from me? I thought frozen dinners meant the old three-compartment foil-wrapped numbers on which I'd overdosed during my first job. If I never see another Swanson's Chicken Dinner, it'll be too soon. But nowadays there are dinners for the microwave, *mirabile dictu,* and the entrees are simply unbelievable. There are things like Oriental chicken and vegetables, complete turkey dinners, various seafood dishes, pasta prepared with about a zillion sauces, and more vegetables than I've even heard of. There was even microwaveable *soup,* for heaven's sake. How would a person choose? After much deliberation, I selected a gaily packaged Shrimp Creole Dinner, hefting it doubtfully. It seemed rather small, and decidedly light, so I took one more. After all, I told myself on the way to the check-out counter, this *was* supper. And I needed to fortify myself for my evening meeting with CLAW.

I unpacked the Shrimp Creole Dinner, and left it on the counter while I went in search of my microwave. Payment-in-kind from a former client, this electronic gizmo had resided in my spare room for two years. I never could figure out what to use it for. Well, its time had come. I wrestled it out of its cardboard and styrofoam nest, and carried it into the kitchen, looking for a place it could call home. Over by my Krups coffeemaker seemed a likely location, so I put it down, plugged it in, then stood back and looked at the sinister bulk of the oven. To tell the truth, one of the reasons I had never unpacked my microwave was that the idea of it made me nervous. What were microwaves, anyhow, and how could they cook food so fast? Hibachis I could understand. Stoves made sense. Even toaster ovens were comprehensible to me. But microwaves? Didn't the Voice of America travel around the world on microwaves?

Feeling like a technological dolt, I unwrapped my shrimp dinner and read the directions. I placed the dinner in the maw of the oven, closed the door, set the timer, and swallowed nervously. Things were in the hands of the gods now. Waiting for a sonic boom, or a flash of light, I pressed the COOK panel. Nothing more disturbing than a gentle hum emanated. Gathering my courage, I peered in through the little window on the door. The glass plate was rotating, docilely microwaving the shrimp. I chuckled, feeling inordinately proud of myself. Ain't technology grand?

In four minutes, a buzzer sounded, and I removed the bubbling delicacy, depositing it on the table. In the intervening three minutes, I had fished a mismatched knife and fork out of the drawer, tossed a paper napkin onto the table, and found a reasonably clean placemat onto which to put this feast. Never let it be said that I'm not a classy diner.

As I had suspected, the shrimp was delicious. I was hooked — I knew it. On my microwave, and on these tasty little dishes. I thought guiltily of my bill — $7.89 for two Shrimp Creole Dinners. Who did I think I was? The Prime Minister? Oh well, I rationalized, maybe I could recycle the microwave plates and use them for Repo's food. Fat chance. Once Repo got a whiff of this, the only way he would accept the plastic plates was if they included the original dinner. Thinking fondly of the furry gray footwarmer, I decided to save the other shrimp dinner for him. Just this once I told myself. A welcome home present. Something to perk up his appetite.

I put my utensils in the sink, then headed for the bedroom. Disguising myself for the CLAW meeting was going to take all my ingenuity.

* * * * *

I walked across the church parking lot, noting with surprise that there seemed to be at least two dozen cars parked there. CLAW had certainly gotten the word out. And that was good, because I had no great confidence in my ability to fool Judith and Liz for very long. I'm too tall, and my hair is the wrong color. Even though I was still wearing the sunglasses and the Canucks cap I had worn this afternoon, and had dressed in a nondescript pair of jeans, a navy turtleneck and my windbreaker, I had little confidence that I could go undetected for long.

I followed the signs and found myself in the church basement — a large, drafty, dimly lighted room with doorways leading to smaller rooms on my left and right. The smell of coffee and the murmur of voices off to my right persuaded me that I was in the proper place. Giving the bill of my cap a firm tug, I moseyed on into the meeting.

Judith and Liz were busy sorting through a pile of papers at the front of the room and I took a seat in the back, directly behind a pillar. After all, I didn't want to see, I wanted to hear.

"Hi, there," a cheery voice called from beside me.

I turned cautiously.

"I'm Green Heron," a freckled little sandy-haired woman said, taking a seat beside me.

"I'm, um, er, Cat," I told her in a burst of inspiration.

"I thought you were a new one." When I said nothing, she frowned. "You are, aren't you? I didn't see you on the action committee last time."

"Er, yes," I said, hoping she wouldn't insist I leave just yet. "I hoped it wasn't too late to join up."

She grimaced a little. "You must have seen the notice I put up in the Oak Bay Natural Foods Emporium. I shouldn't have done that. This meeting isn't really for new members."

"Oh," I said, thinking furiously. "Too bad. And I was really looking forward to the action." I bent toward her conspiratorially. "I'm a Ninth Life dropout. They're too tame for me. I want to get into the trenches," I improvised. "Rough stuff doesn't bother me. Especially when it's for a good cause."

She looked at me speculatively. "Yes, you just might do. You say you were a Ninth Lifer?"

"Well, not an active one," I equivocated. "You could check me out with the president — Alison Bell."

"I guess you're all right," she said. "And if you want action, you've come to the right place. Judith and Liz have terrific plans for this Saturday."

"Yeah — the Day of Shame," I said. "That's what attracted me to CLAW."

"You might be just what Derek needs," she told me. "He's organizing the Liberation Squad. I'll introduce you."

Liberation Squad? Give me strength. "Derek?"

"Yeah, the guy in the leather jacket. Up front."
I followed her finger. Derek, a thin, dark-haired guy in a camouflage jacket and khaki pants with about a million pockets, was deep in consultation with a small group of men and women on one side of the room. "Thanks," I told Green Heron. "If it's okay with you, I'd like to listen for a while, then check in with Derek." But one or two of the things she mentioned had started me thinking. I decided to ask a few questions.

"How many meetings have I missed?" A roundabout way of finding out how old CLAW was.

"Oh, four, maybe five. We're pretty new on the scene. Mostly Greenpeace dropouts, brought together by Liz. We've been talking about forming a lab animal liberation group for a long time, and CLAW just sort of fell into place. Liz found the cause for us — the rabbits at Living World — we supplied the personpower, and here we are, ready to go. We'll get some good press out of this."

Great, I thought. Riding into media stardom on the coattails of Ninth Life. The organization that did all the donkey work — the patient planning, the documenting, the legal groundwork, the scientific opinions. And good old Liz had been plotting CLAW shenanigans for a month, had she? That was just about the time when Mary went undercover at Living World. Very interesting. I gave up believing in coincidences when I gave up believing in the Tooth Fairy, and this fortuitous conjunction of events stank. I filed it for later consideration and turned my attention back to Green Heron.

"Have you let the media know?" I asked.

She burst out laughing. "God, no. They'll be told at the last minute — Friday night."

"Friday? I thought the Day of Shame was Saturday?"

"It is," she said, looking sly, "but we're not waiting for Saturday. Liz says Living World will probably have the entire Saanich police force around the place on Saturday. No, we're striking on Friday night."

I thought of the bargain Liz had made with Alison, and shook my head in disgust. What this babe wanted more than anything was to make a media splash, it seemed. To stage a coup. An event. Liberators, my eye.

"Hello, Caitlin," a voice said sweetly behind me.

I turned, knowing perfectly well who would be there. Tweedledum and Tweedledee. Judith and Liz.

"Evening, ladies," I said.

Green Heron looked at them apprehensively, blinked, then suddenly realized that she had just been terribly indiscreet. "But isn't she . . . I mean she said she was . . ."

"It's all right," Liz said with uncharacteristic kindness. "Why don't you go finalize assignments for the billboard with Suzi and her group. We'll talk to Caitlin."

Eyes wide, Green Heron hurried off.

"You made a deal with Alison," I said, judging it best to go on the offensive. "She trusted you. You lied to her. You never had any intentions of waiting until Saturday."

"Damn that blabbermouth," Judith said heatedly.

"Never mind," Liz said. "She couldn't have

blabbed much because she doesn't know much. I learned that from Alison," she told me, twisting her lips in an unpleasant smile.

I decided that for what it was worth, I was going to play this straight. "Why not stop this silly competition?" I asked. "Isn't that what this is all about — one-upmanship? Why not ask Alison to consider, just consider, the kinds of things you have in mind. The action-oriented things. But be straight with her. I can't believe there isn't a place for you in Ninth Life. They need activists — I completely agree with you. But you need the background on the local companies, and the legal and administrative help that a national organization could provide. You could be a very effective team."

"No," Liz said flatly.

I felt exasperated. "Just no?"

"That's right. You don't understand a thing about this, Miss high-and-mighty Detective Caitlin Reece," she said scathingly. "Why don't you stick to finding lost dogs or spying on cheating husbands or whatever it is you do?" She snorted a little in laughter. "How could someone like you possibly understand what we're trying to do? What have you ever believed in, put your head on the chopping block for? You're nothing but a whore. Someone for hire."

"Oh I am, am I?" I replied, stung by her insults. "The only difference between your victims and mine is that yours are animals and mine are humans."

She hooted with laughter. "What a pile of crap. I don't know what you're talking about."

"Dammit, Liz, you know exactly what I'm talking about. We're doing the same job."

She frowned ferociously, but didn't interrupt. Was it possible that a seedling was taking root in the granite boulder of her mind? Finally she looked away. "Maybe so," she said. "But we're on different sides this time."

"But why?" I wanted to shake her. As I saw it, only her ego prevented her from delivering this activist organization to Alison where it could be sensibly incorporated into Ninth Life's plans. CLAW, it seemed, was *her* brainchild, and she was not going to give it up. "If your group and Alison's teamed up, I'd even throw in my time and expertise to help you get the goods on Living World," I offered. "Wouldn't you like to see things done properly? I know people in the television business. The Crown Prosecutor's office, too. You could get real media attention. Responsible coverage of a real issue. And you could nail Living World for violations of laws that are already on the books. Why not do things the right way?"

For a reply, she glared at me. Man, was this tough. She was about as impenetrable as an iceberg. I wondered suddenly if this was purely an ego thing with Liz or if there was something more to it. Something, say, between Liz and Alison. Something Alison hadn't told me about. Or something else altogether. There had to be some very compelling reason for her to be so adamant, and I was beginning to doubt that the spurious glory of heading an animal liberation cadre was all of it.

I had one card left, and I decided to play it. "What about Mary?" I asked, knowing it was a low blow. "Mary might have died for this cause. She was your friend — or at least a coworker in a common endeavor. Don't you want to see this handled right? For her sake?"

Judith made a strangled noise and lunged for me. To my surprise, Liz grabbed her arm and stepped between us. She took another step toward me so we were standing literally toe to toe. The proximity made me uncomfortable — I hate close work. But I was pleased to note that Liz had to tilt her head back to look at me. Height hath its advantages.

"You're lucky I don't have some of the guys throw you out of here," she said in a low voice. "But I have more important things to do than mess with you. So I want you to turn around and walk out. Quietly. No fuss. No more crap about principles or joining Ninth Life."

"You know, you're one unreasonable lady," I told her. "If I go quietly — don't make a fuss so your followers won't start asking questions — what do I get in return? As I see it, you'll owe me."

"What do you get in return?" she asked incredulously. "Nothing. Why should I give you anything?"

I shrugged. "Somehow I thought we were all in this together. You, Alison, me. That we had a common enemy — Maleck."

She breathed heavily, opening and closing her fists.

"Silly me," I told her. Then I did what she wanted. Quietly, without a fuss, I turned and left.

* * * * *

128

"That was masterful," I told myself aloud in disgust as I drove out the Saanich Highway to Emma's. "You really didn't learn much, and you let that egomaniacal little twerp walk all over you."

I couldn't disagree with myself, so I clammed up. But I had learned one extremely useful thing — that CLAW intended to do its dastardly deed on Friday night. So I had one less day to bring down the walls of Jericho. Let's see — this was Tuesday. Lester and I were due at Living World tomorrow. I'd certainly better have a bright idea in the next two days. I knew what I wanted to accomplish — to present Val with a videotape of what was *really* going on at Living World. But I wasn't at all sure how I was going to get that tape made. And certainly not in the next two days. In order to defuse CLAW, I had to get the tape to Val by Friday so it could air Friday night. Not Saturday night.

Then I thought of something that made me snort in disgust. Did I really believe that Liz would keep her word? Did I really believe that once I got something concrete on Living World, something that we could air Friday night, something that Ninth Life could use in court, that Liz would see to it that CLAW behaved itself? That she would call off whatever shenanigans she had planned for Friday? Fat chance. She seemed to be the sort of person to whom oath-breaking was of no consequence. And lying to me evidently didn't seem to rate with her as one of the seven deadly sins. But what about lying to Alison? What *was* going on with Liz, anyhow? For Alison's sake, and Ninth Life's, too, I decided I really ought to find out.

Chapter 9

"Depressed?" I shouted at Emma Neely. "How can he possibly be depressed? He's a cat! One of God's chosen creatures. A day of tests, a hundred and eighty dollars in bills, and this is your diagnosis? Depression? Give me a break! I could have consulted a witch doctor for less. And maybe gotten the same results. I'll tell you who's depressed — *I'm* depressed!"

The patient favored me with a pernicious yellow gaze. Emma looked at me reproachfully. Ginny gave me a smoldering stare she probably saved for animal abusers. All this combined disapproval worked. I felt like a worm.

"Caitlin," Emma said soothingly, "believe me, I know what I'm talking about. There's not a thing wrong with him, physically."

"But . . ."

"But logic dictates that there's a reason for his aberrant behavior."

"Hmmph," I opined. "It could just be feline perversity, couldn't it?"

"There's no such thing," Ginny said hotly. "There are only dumb feline owners."

Emma gave Ginny a "better humor the client" look, and she subsided.

I didn't understand. "Are you saying that Repo's gone around the bend? Emma, cats just don't get *depressed*."

Repo did not dignify these remarks with so much as a twitch of a whisker. I noted, however, that he did arrange his ears in Stealth Bomber configuration — a sign of incipient bad humor. Not a good omen. I could now look forward to a really enthusiastic feline manicure performed on the back of my armchair.

"Take Repo back to his cage, why don't you, Ginny?" Emma suggested. With a flounce of her braids, Ginny scooped Repo up and marched into the back room, doubtless to commiserate with him about the mental capacity of his owner.

"Ginny will take care of Repo," Emma said. "C'mon into my office. We're closed, so we can chat a little. And not about Repo, either. About you, and why I only see you once a year."

I followed Emma's white-coated shape into her office — a cubbyhole only big enough to contain her battered, secondhand desk and filing cabinet. She opened the filing cabinet and began to stuff manila folders inside, giving me time to compose my answer.

Why *did* she only see me once a year? I stood morosely, hands in pockets, looking out the window at the dark autumn sky. It was just eight o'clock, but all the light was gone from the day. Now it seemed as though we were in limbo, trapped in an eerie slate-colored world which was neither day nor night. The rain which had threatened since afternoon had finally begun in earnest, and slipped down the glass like separate streams of tears.

"It's not just you, Em," I told her, deciding on the truth. "I'm no good at . . . continuity. I don't get around to seeing people as often as I should."

She took off her white vet's smock and hung it on a coatrack, then took a seat in the chair behind her desk. Running a hand through her curly hair, she looked at me levelly. "Well, I think it's a damned shame. What're you afraid of?"

Opening a drawer she plunked a bottle of Chivas Regal on the desk. "I've had a rotten day," she said, offering me a paper cup. "Want a drink?"

"Thanks," I said, and she poured us both healthy belts. I sniffed mine appreciatively before I drank, savoring the peaty undertones. I swallowed a mouthful, and it burned all the way down. I thought about what she had said. "I don't want to be . . . disappointed, Em," I told her. "People always let me down."

She waved a hand impatiently. "Panther piss.

That's a cop-out, Reece. Nobody's perfect — you know that. Try again."

I sighed. "Oh, hell, I don't know. Intimacy is a crock — it's just too hard."

"Better," she said.

"Besides, I've been told I have serious character flaws."

"What, you too?"

I smiled. "Yeah, me too. But seriously, Em, I've heard these criticisms often enough to wonder if there isn't something to them."

"Like what?"

"Well, I'm not a nurturing individual, for one."

"True."

"Hmmph. Let's see — I wisecrack my way through life, for another."

"Also true."

I groaned. "Em, give me a break. I thought you were on my side."

"I am," she said, lacing her hands together behind her head. "Go on."

"I act too tough."

"Mmm, 'too tough' is debatable. But tough is the right adjective, all right. So, is there anything else?"

"I guess that's it," I said.

She sighed. "Well, life hasn't sweetened you any. You've always been a non-nurturing, wisecracking, tough-talking broad. I'd add egocentric, too, if I were doing the criticizing. But that's about it. Those aren't hanging offenses in my books. You're a hell of a lot of fun to be around. And all that tough stuff hides a marshmallow heart. Haven't any of your critics discovered that?"

I cleared my throat a little self-consciously. "Um, well, no. I guess they got turned off before they discovered my redeeming characteristics."

"Rat spit! More likely, you kicked them out of bed at the first whisper of criticism. Perserverence was never your style."

I glared at her. "You sure think you know me pretty well, don't you?"

She chuckled. "Caitlin, dear, you shared my house for two long years. Yeah, I think I know you pretty well."

I took another swallow of Scotch and closed my eyes, leaning back in my chair. "You're right."

"So what's up?" she asked. "Is this just non-specific middle-aged angst, or does it have a focus?"

"Nope," I said, sighing. "No focus. Just ennui, I guess."

"Ennui, my aunt Fanny," she snorted. "It's that rotten job of yours."

I glanced at her appraisingly. Em was another one of the few people who knew what I really did for a living. I tell most people I'm a legal consultant and that does it. They must figure it's about as interesting as being an accountant, or plumber, or an endodontist, because they never ask any more questions. "Oh? What's wrong with my job?"

"Caitlin, be serious! The only people you ever see are people in trouble. And to get them out of that trouble, you usually end up breaking about half a dozen laws, lying, cheating, stealing, being the heavy." She ran a hand through her hair again. "It's bad for your self-image. Not to mention your blood pressure. And you're always broke because half your clients stiff you —"

"Now, now," I interrupted. "They make payments-in-kind."

"Pig poop they do. And these clients are always under some terrible deadline — you know, find the missing family silver in forty-eight hours *or else.*" She finished her Scotch and tossed the cup in the trash. "It's not a good way to live, Caitlin. Your outlook on life can't help but be rotten."

"So you're saying that I have lowered expectation levels?"

"Yeah, I am. And when people live down to your expectations — you know, when they're critical of the suit of armor you think you have to wear to hide your vulnerable side — you say 'Ha, that's about what I expected,' and off you run."

I finished the rest of my Scotch and tossed my cup after Emma's. "What the hell, you could be right," I told her. "How did we get into all this encounter-group falderal anyhow?"

"I just asked you why I didn't see you anymore."

"Hmmmf," I said. "Are you enlightened?"

"A little." She smiled. "You ought to give people more of a chance. Some of us might even come through for you."

"I know," I sighed. "I'm working on it." I felt bad. Emma was my friend and I'd neglected her. I stood up. "I'll try to be better, Em."

"Okay," she told me. "And try not to take on every client who comes and cries on your shoulder. Surely there are other people who wear white hats. Other people in the monster-slaying business."

135

I tried a grin, and it felt pretty feeble. Why argue about it? Em was concerned about me. I wasn't about to tell her that I didn't know anyone else in the business of rescuing, thwarting, or interdicting. That I had a hard time turning people down who came to me for help — particularly women who had already been folded, spindled, and mutilated. Who were, in most cases, at the end of their resources, their prospects, and their wits. So I let it go.

"Sure," I said. "I'll tell them to look in the Yellow Pages."

"So, what about Repo?" she asked me. "Incidentally, you might as well leave him here tonight. Ginny will have him all settled in by now."

"Well, all right," I said reluctantly. "So he's depressed, is he? Do you have some suggestions for treatment?"

"As a matter of fact, I do."

Uh oh. I was afraid I was about to get an earful. "Shoot."

"I don't think you spend enough time with him. He needs stimulation. Now that you don't let him roam the neighborhood — which is a good thing, don't misunderstand me — he needs something to take the place of his daily rounds."

"Something like what?"

"Well, a neighborhood child could come in and play with him."

"Nope. No kids in my neighborhood."

"Okay, how about a senior citizen?"

"Emma, c'mon. I can't run a daycare center for the benefit of my cat. My hours are too irregular. Sometimes I have to sleep in the daytime. I don't want cat calisthenics going in the parlor."

136

"Okay," she said calmly. "You're going to love this next suggestion."

"I bet."

"Get him a friend."

"A friend? What do you mean?"

"Another cat."

"Another cat? Oh, sure. Emma, I used to see Repo with his neighborhood 'friends.' They'd arch and hiss and mince around on their toes exchanging blood-curdling insults, then they'd rip pieces out of each others' pelts. Repo bit one of his friends' ears clean off! No way do I want feline Armageddon in my living room."

"Get him a kitten."

"A what? Absolutely not. He'd have the kitten for breakfast."

"Trust me. He wouldn't."

"Why not?"

"Because neutered adult cats accept kittens very well. I've never known one who had a kitten for breakfast."

I stopped and considered this. "You mean they won't fight?"

"Well, Repo will have to explain to the kitten who's boss, but after a few cuffs everything should be all right."

"Hmmm," I said. "And you think this will cure Repo of his depression? Make him start eating again? Get him back to his old self?"

"I think so. But I'm not an expert in the field of cat psychology. You might do well to consult someone who is, before you take such a big step." She fished around in her desk drawer and handed me a business card. In neat calligraphy, it read:

The address and phone number were printed underneath.

I smiled. Gray's reputation was spreading. "Thanks," I said. "I might just do that. I'll come by for Repo tomorrow."

She walked me to the door and opened the door for me. "Hey," she said.

I turned. "What?"

"Don't stay away so long next time. Neither of us is getting any younger. Hell, I could even be persuaded to cook dinner."

I raised an eyebrow. Emma's dinners were a long-standing joke between us. A cook she was not. "You're on," I said. "How about next week?"

"I'll get out my cookbooks. Bye, Caitlin."

Chapter 10

Alison's house in James Bay was absolutely dark.
With a quick stab of disappointment, I looked at my
watch — almost eleven. Had she given up on me and
gone to bed? Darn, I knew I should have phoned
from the highway. But I hadn't wanted to brave the
rain. I yawned, wondering if I should leave a note
and go on home to bed, or get out of the car and
roust Alison out of *her* bed.

Across the street, out past the sea wall, the moon
sailed in and out of ragged scraps of cloud. By its
fitful light I could see the dark ocean undulating as if

it were a sea beast plagued with bad dreams. A gusty wind blew the rain in little flurries against the windshield, and I shivered, vowing to get my heater fixed before winter.

As I sat in the driveway, idling my motor and my brain, a light went on in an upstairs window, and a curtain was twitched aside. That looked promising. I switched off the motor and waited for lights to come on downstairs. When they did, I sprinted from the car to the front door. Never let it be said that a little inclement weather can deter me. No sirree.

"Caitlin," Alison said with evident pleasure. "I thought you wouldn't make it tonight."

"Surprise," I said, my teeth chattering. For someone who had just been rousted out of bed, she looked wonderful. She had pulled on a blue and gray tartan robe over a pair of pale blue pajamas. Her hair was a little tousled, and the dark smudges under her eyes gave her a vulnerable, waif-like look that I found immensely touching.

"Come on in," she said, smiling.

I did, and stood shivering a little in the front hall while Alison locked the door.

"You're frozen," she said. "Come on into the living room. I'll build up the fire, and you can make your report." She looked back over her shoulder and grinned. "Isn't that what detectives do? Report to their clients?"

"Absolutely," I said.

I stood uncertainly in the middle of the floor, looking at the piles of paper on the round brass coffee table. It must be hard not to be able to carry forward the work you believe in, I thought. Well, maybe I could get CLAW off Alison's back and let her get back to work.

"What have you been up to?" I asked.

She stirred around the embers and tossed a log on the fire, closing the screen, and brushing off her hands. "I'm planning how to resurrect Ninth Life," she told me. "We need a new Executive Committee. I've been going through the roster of members, trying to decide who to approach."

"What about Ian?" I asked, suddenly recalling I hadn't seen his motorcycle in the driveway. "He seems a natural. Is he staying?"

"He's a very steadying influence," she said. "I hope he stays. But he's awfully pessimistic. I just . . . don't know."

"Where is he?"

She shrugged. "Out somewhere. He comes and goes at odd hours. Also, he's been drinking too much."

I thought about the chat I had had with him in the Dog and Pony and felt disappointed. A steadying influence, eh?

"And what about you?" I asked. "How have you been?"

She put her hands in the pockets of her robe. "Oh, all right, I guess. I just won't let myself believe the end of Ninth LIfe is around the corner." She looked at me gravely. "I'm counting on you, Caitlin."

"I know," I told her.

She sighed. "Listen, can I get you something? Coffee? Tea? A drink? Maybe something to eat —

there's a tray of cheese and crackers and fruit one of the local Ninth Life members brought over. I really didn't feel like having any of it earlier."

"Sounds great," I said honestly. "And some Scotch if you have any."

"Sure," she said. "Come on out to the kitchen and help."

She carried the tray, a couple of paper plates and napkins, and I brought Scotch and glasses. We deposited everything on the coffee table.

"Okay," I said, piling a Carr's Water Cracker with a redolent mound of Stilton, "time for my report." I munched a little, organizing my thoughts, then began. "I have a plan," I said. "A friend of mine at Channel Twenty-two has agreed to air a tape of whatever I can get showing what's happening at Living World."

She gasped. "Caitlin! That's wonderful. But . . . how will you get the tape?"

"I'm not one hundred percent sure, yet," I said, "but I'm going to Living World tomorrow. I'm posing as a television reporter interviewing Maleck."

"My God," she said. "You do move fast. But you realize of course, that you won't be shown anything useful. You'll get the white glove tour — all the skeletons will be hidden away in the closet."

"I know," I told her, "but after I leave Living World at least I'll know where the closet is."

She was quiet for a moment, and then the import of what I had just said hit her. "Caitlin, you're . . . you're going to *break in*. Make the tape yourself!"

I said nothing, piling a Digestive Biscuit with rat trap cheddar.

"You are, aren't you?"

"Well, not completely by myself — after all, we

want the tape to turn out. My role will be more that of executive producer. But, yeah, I'll be there. And here's a new wrinkle," I told her. "The deadline has been moved up. I learned from CLAW — quite inadvertently, I might add — that the little shindig they plan to hold at Living World will be Friday night. Not Saturday."

"But Liz gave me her word!" Alison was indignant.

"Yup."

"Damn her!"

"You can say that again."

She turned to me, her eyes angry. "But it's impossible. You'll never do it in time." Thwarted, disappointed, she aimed her anger at me. "Dammit, Caitlin!"

I swallowed the last of my cracker, took a sip of Scotch, and clasped my hands in front of me. I understood what she was saying. But I thought I ought to set her straight. "We're not beaten yet," I told her quietly. "I don't know about you, but I don't lie down and die when things get tough. I believe in redundancy. The videotape isn't our only hope. I've got several plans underway, and a whole bunch of people helping me. It gives us an edge, Alison. That way if one plan bombs, well, there's still hope." I shrugged. "So the deadline has been moved up. So what? We'll all just work a little faster."

She nodded. "I'm sorry. I should have known you had contingency plans. That you'd know how to allow for emergencies like this." She looked up at me and smiled. "Tonia said you were extremely resourceful. It's just that, forgive me, I've never known anyone like you."

Anyone like me. I wondered what that meant. I waited for her to continue.

"You're so . . . direct. Nothing seems to daunt you. You figure out what you want, map out three different ways of getting there, and attack on all fronts at once." She shook her head. "You're amazing."

"Please," I said, more than a little embarrassed. "We're not home free yet. Let's wait until Friday before you get too excited."

"All right," she said, her eyes silver in the firelight, an unreadable expression on her face.

I sighed, sorrier than hell that I had to break the mood. But it was late, I was tired, and I had one more thing to report. "Now," I said, "about Mary."

"What have you found out?" she asked eagerly.

"The night she tossed the film and the cat into the dumpster — Sunday — I saw a light-colored late-model car follow her out of the parking lot. After I heard about her accident, I remembered that car. Today I got into the Police Impound Lot and examined her car. There was a long smear of light yellow paint on the fender. She'd been sideswiped. Probably run off the road."

Alison pressed her lips together tightly.

"Tomorrow, I plan to get a look at the car that sideswiped her."

"At Living World."

"Right. Probably no one's done anything yet about the dent in *its* bodywork. Or the VW's paint which is undoubtedly in the dent. As well, I got the first three letters of the license plate on Sunday. If the paint and the license match, I'm turning the evidence over to a friend of mine who'll see it gets to Metro. I've made an inquiry about her blood alcohol count, too, and if she hadn't been drinking — and she sure hadn't when I talked to her — I think there's enough evidence to open an investigation. For murder."

"Murder," she said, as if she'd never really understood the word until now. "If we can tie Evan Maleck to Mary's murder, well, that will be the end of it. Of him and of Living World. Finally." She looked at me, her eyes flinty. "We'd have them! Not even Maleck could run away from something like that."

I didn't want to disillusion her, but I wanted her to face facts. "There are a lot of 'ifs' in what you've just said. Justice moves slowly, and sometimes —" I grimaced, "it doesn't move in the ways you or I might expect. Justice is a disappointing mistress. I know — I served her for seven long years. That's why, now, I prefer to be more . . . self-sufficient. To have lots of irons in the fire. Waiting for justice can be a lot like waiting for the Second Coming." I smiled, trying not to make more of this than I needed to. "You know — praise the Lord and pass the ammunition."

"You're right," she said, wiping her eyes with the back of her hand. I saw the sparkle of tears on her eyelashes and resisted the impulse to brush them away. Not now, I told myself. Do your job. Concentrate.

"Well," I said heartily, "end of report." I looked wistfully at the remnants of the cheese tray and stood up. "If I'm to be any good at all tomorrow, I'd better drag myself home to my bed."

"Caitlin," she said, "there's one more thing."

145

"Oh?"

"When Judith was here today, when she was struggling with what she had to tell me, she said something very odd."

"Tell me."

I saw Alison take a deep breath. "She said, 'You'll never forgive me if I don't tell you about Mary. But if I do, you'll never forgive me either.' Then she said just one more word."

"What word?"

"Just 'Liz.' Nothing more. She started crying then, and ran out of the house."

I sat back down thoughtfully. Liz, eh? And Judith was worrying about forgiveness. I thought I knew what they added up to. I looked over at Alison, not wanting to say this. But it had to be said. "I think Living World planted a spy on you," I told her, not knowing any way to make it easier. "And I think that spy was Liz. I believe she betrayed Mary to Living World and that Judith came to know about it. And now that knowledge is eating Judith up."

Alison just looked at me, appalled. Then she shook her head. "Liz betraying Mary — that makes sense if she *was* planted on us as a spy. But what about the rest of it? She started CLAW."

I massaged my eyes, trying to force my tired brain to work. "Let's try to think this through. So she started CLAW. So what? All CLAW will do is stage some sensational event and alienate everyone who values private property rights. Living World will end up looking like the good guys." I got up and began to pace. "The woman is like a loose cannon. She's setting up a whole lot of people to take a fall. If she succeeds, she'll have single-handedly set your cause back years."

There was a tiny something that wasn't quite right about this, but the more I talked, the tinier it got. Yeah, the whole thing made a certain kind of sense. Living World couldn't answer Ninth Life's accusations directly, so they had to be indirect. Make an end run. Hamstring them. Plant a spy. A fifth columnist. Liz.

"Now what?" Alison asked.

"I don't know," I confessed. "I've already had a go-round with Liz. But now I don't feel so bad that she couldn't be appealed to. Of course she couldn't — she's playing for the other team." But then I realized that I knew someone who wasn't. Well, not completely, anyhow. Someone who was so consumed with guilt about what she knew that she had come to Alison wanting to confess. Judith. The weak link. And weak links could often be broken. "Say, do you know where Judith and Liz are living now?" I asked.

Alison shook her head. "No."

My heart sank. Of course not. That would have been too easy.

"But Judith left me her phone number."

"She did? Do you have it?"

"Yes. It's in the kitchen."

I stood up. "May I have it?"

"All right," Alison said and preceded me to the kitchen. She copied a number from a notepad by the phone and handed it to me. "But you still don't have the address," she said. "And I'm sure the number is unlisted."

"I can get it," I said. This would take Francis all

147

of thirty seconds. And cost me another hundred. But I thought it could be useful. Useful in what way, I wasn't sure. What would I do with the address, anyhow? Wait for Liz at her house, truss her like a chicken and lock her in a cupboard until Saturday? It wasn't a bad idea but I didn't think it would help. Liz, too, would have set wheels in motion by now, and I was willing to bet that they would roll along quite nicely without her. Still, I wanted that address. "I'll think of something to use it for," I told Alison with more confidence than I felt.

She walked me to the door, and I turned to face her in the narrow hall.

"Be careful," she said, her eyes worried. Suddenly, unbelievably, she stepped toward me and put her arms around my waist. "I'm frightened, Caitlin," she said. "The idea of betrayal, it . . . scares the hell out of me."

My arms came up around her of their own accord. Her head, I noted, fit just under my cheekbone, and her hair, which was tickling my nose, smelled like summer.

"You feel so solid and substantial," she told me, holding me tightly.

"Er, well, yes . . ." I muttered, patting her shoulder, then smoothing her hair.

She sighed, and moved her head so it fit more neatly under my cheekbone. That was fine. It was her hands which had moved inside my jacket and up under my turtleneck which were giving me fits. My stomach felt as though the bottom had fallen out of it, and I realized that my mind was well on its way to being a perfect blank.

It was clear that something was expected of me,

something more than just sisterly pats — Alison's hands on my back were telling me that. And I wasn't unwilling — hell, she had been the subject of concupiscent thoughts for days now — but I wanted to know who she thought I was. Caitlin Reece? Any solid, substantial body? Or the ghost of Mary? But how could I ask the question? Fortunately, I didn't have to.

The deadbolt turned with a *clack* and the front door opened suddenly behind me, whacking me smartly in the back of the head. "Ow!" I exclaimed, returning painfully to reality.

Alison jumped back, away from me, and I followed her. We both turned to look at the opening door. Belatedly I thought about my .357 reposing uselessly in its shoebox.

"Hey, it's just me," a voice called. Someone poked a head through the partly opened doorway, someone with dark hair that fell over his forehead in a wing. "Everything okay?" Ian asked.

"Your timing is lousy," I told him on my way out. "But thanks."

Chapter 11

I sank into the softness of my mattress with a
grateful sigh. Pulling the comforter up to my armpits,
I sipped my Scotch, then reached for the yellow tablet
I kept beside my bed. It surely couldn't hurt to do a
little recapitulation, a little noting down of where I
was, where I thought I was going, and how I thought
I was going to get there. I scribbled "Living World"
on my notepad, then yawned hugely, deciding I was
too tired to do any writing after all. Well, I'd lie here
and think, anyhow.

So what did I need? Some revealing video footage

taken in Living World's labs. Simple enough. A little breaking and entering should get me what I wanted. Lester and I would reconnoiter the place tomorrow, then later on at night we'd come back. I'd go in first to silence the alarms, locate the lab, and open a back door, then in would pop Lester. He'd shoot as much footage as we had time for, then we'd both beat it back to town and I'd hand over the videotape to Val. Simple, right?

I squirmed on my pillow, trying to get more comfortable. Simple? Hardly. There were about a hundred things that could go wrong. The more I thought about it, the less feasible the plan became.

I finished the rest of my Scotch, yawned again, then turned off the light. Just who was this Evan Maleck, I wondered as I slid down the inky incline of sleep. What kind of *creature* was he? The thought of confronting someone like him, someone intelligent yet willfully immoral, made me feel ill. I'd seen my share of Evan Malecks — people who knew the difference between right and wrong and simply chose to do the latter. I wasn't looking forward to the confrontation. Another thought nagged at me, a bubble rising to the top of memory's pond, but it was too much trouble to try to figure out what it was. I fell into welcome darkness.

* * * * *

Darkness. What was I doing down here in the cellar in the middle of the night? I tried my best to remember how I had gotten here, but panic made me witless. Stumbling blindly forward, hands outstretched, I searched for the light switch which I knew must be on the wall at the bottom of the stairs. I had started to sweat, and wondered if the sharp, coppery smell was my own fear. I didn't care. I had to have light. Light to see by. Light to help me get out of here. Before she became aware of my presence and came for me. The Dark Lady. Gibbering in fear, I found the light switch. My fingers fumbled with it, then flipped it on . . . Nothing happened.

"No!" I cried out, putting my hands over my face. Then I heard it — furtive scrabbling in the darkness behind me — the first sounds of pursuit — and fear made me reckless. Staggering forward, I cracked my shin painfully against the bottom step of the staircase. Then, on hands and knees, I scrambled upwards, away from her, away from this dark place. Away.

She caught me halfway up the stairs, and I felt her icy hand close on my ankle. "Caitlinnnn," she breathed. "At last."

* * * * *

Screaming my head off, I awoke to find myself in my own bed. Teeth chattering, I snapped on the bedside light just to make sure. I threw my comforter aside, and hauled myself upright. The Dark Lady. I peeled off my sodden clothes and tossed them into the closet. Oh goody. My *bête noir.* I took a clean sweatshirt and sweatpants out of my bottom drawer and pulled them on thoughtfully. I hadn't dreamed about the Dark Lady for almost a year.

Sighing, I padded out into the kitchen and set a pan of milk heating for hot chocolate. While it warmed, I sat at the kitchen table and brooded.

152

The Dark Lady was my psyche's manifestation of the Llewelyn prescience. The females in our family — the Llewelyns — seem to be cursed with knowing more than they should. Or more than they want to. Some of them went wacko — certifiably round the bend. My mother's two sisters had long ago stopped trying to make sense of their so-called gift, and now existed in fantasy worlds of their own. My Aunt Fiona had succumbed first to madness, and then death. Other Llewelyn women, however, had made an accommodation with their prescience. I was one of the latter.

Reconciling myself to this essential difference between me and other people had not been an easy job. It had caused me a lot of problems as a teenager. But now that I had come to terms with this second sight, I found I could always count on two things. One was that, in times of extraordinary stress, my brain just seemed to kick into overdrive, to sizzle, and I "knew" the answers to crucial questions. I suddenly knew facts I ought not to know. Essential facts. Facts I could have no possible way of knowing.

The other thing I could count on was a visit from the Dark Lady. I thought of it as a psychic burglar alarm. A sign from my psyche that I ought to operate in Code Blue. That I ought to be very, very careful. It had taken half a dozen dreams like the one I had just had before I made the connection, but now I recognized this psychic visitation for what it was — a warning. I, too, had somehow come to know more than I should, and the Dark Lady's visit was my right brain trying to communicate this fact to my left brain.

A warning. I stood up to make the hot chocolate,

153

thinking this over. Okay. I would just have to be extra careful in my dealings with Living World. Presumably the Dark Lady would like it better if I earned my living making pots or selling real estate. Then I might not hear from her so often.

And I decided one other thing, too. I was definitely not taking Lester into Living World's labs with me. I'd make my midnight video myself.

I took the cocoa back to my bedroom, turned off the light and lay there, my hands around its comfortable warmth, sipping it in the dark. Finally, I set the mug down on my bedside table and pulled the comforter up to my nose. As I drifted off into sleep, a memory as bright and ephemeral as a firefly flitted through my mind. It was something to do with another dark place I had dreamed about recently, a place in which I had looked out of eyes that were not my own. But the memory suddenly winked out, and I let it go, too tired to chase it. I'll be careful, I promised. I'll be careful.

WEDNESDAY

Chapter 12

"Hey, Fur Face," I said to Repo as we turned off the highway into Gray's driveway. "You're going to spend some time with Gray. You know — talk to her for a while. We'll go on home after that."

Through the bars of his cage, I could see him washing one hip. He stopped briefly, favored me with a doubtful look, then resumed his ablutions. "Nraaff," he murmured.

"I know, I know," I told him. "So I'm dumb. I admit it. But somehow it never crossed my mind that you might be lonely. After all, you had me."

157

"Yerff," he said, *sotto voce.*

"Right," I agreed. "And a bigger yerf there isn't. Well, let's see what Gray has to say. If you do want a buddy, I'm game. We'll even go the SPCA together. But there's one important matter we'll have to settle first."

"Yang?" he asked.

"You got it — yang. Or will it be yin? You don't have to decide now — just consider it. A lady companion might be, well, mind-expanding. I bet she'd have a whole different viewpoint on life."

The prospect must have rendered him speechless, because he was silent all the way to Gray's door. She had evidently been waiting, for she answered the first knock.

"Repo's ready for his hour of analysis," I told her. "Where's your couch?"

She looked at me reproachfully. "Hello, Repo," she said formally, bending to release him from his cat carrier. "I'm happy to see you. Caitlin will take your traveling compartment into the back room, then I'll give you some breakfast and we'll talk."

Repo rubbed his jowls against the corner of his carrier, evidently delirious with happiness at seeing Gray again. "Ungow?" he asked repeatedly.

"Ungow?" I asked Gray. "That cat has a bigger vocabulary than I do. How do you make sense of all these nrafs and yerfs and yangs and ungows?"

She smiled inscrutably. "Sorry. Proprietary information."

"Yeah, sure." I was skeptical. "Listen, Gray, I'll give you a call later on this afternoon. Should I plan to come and get him tonight?"

"I'm not sure," she said. "Why don't I tell you when you call me?"

"Okay."

For his part, Repo was busy exploring Gray's office. When he came to the cage that contained Jeoffrey, he sat down for a moment, studying the little sleeping cat. Jeoffrey was curled in a tight ball on the seat of the old armchair in his cage. Repo cocked his head to one side, clearly assessing the situation. Then, as if coming to a decision, he stood on his back legs and stretched up the mesh as far as he could reach. Amazed, I saw that he was reaching for the sliding lock to Jeoffrey's cage.

"Hey, Repo, no boy," I told him, going over and patting him. "The little fellow's sick. He needs to be alone."

Repo ignored me. He stretched up the mesh again, uttering a melodious trill. "Frrrittt?" he said softly. "Frrrittt?"

Jeoffrey awakened. He moved his head in the direction of the sound, and I exclaimed when I saw his eyes. The infection seemed to have cleared up — they were only a little runny. But it was their color that was so arresting. They were a pure, brilliant gold, a gold the color of newly minted Canadian Maple Leafs. But it was clear something was wrong because those beautiful gold eyes did not focus on Repo.

"Gray," I said quietly. "Jeoffrey . . . is he . . . can he see?"

"No," she answered.

"Frrritt?" Repo invited again.

"Mmmmm," Jeoffrey replied, stretching out a tentative paw to guide himself down from the chair.

With a sigh, Repo lay down outside Jeoffrey's cage, in much the same way Gray's dogs had laid themselves down the night I had brought the cat to Gray. Arranging himself in tea-cozy position, arms and legs tucked under his body, Repo began a rumbling purr, punctuated with the occasional "Frrrittt."

For his part, Jeoffrey had made his uncertain way over to the door of the cage where Repo lay. He raised his little blind face to Repo's, and through the bars, Repo began to wash him.

"Caitlin, I must go to work now," Gray said, taking a yellow legal pad from her desk and coming over to sit on the floor beside Repo. "I won't see you out. I trust you'll understand."

"I do," I told her, and tiptoed to the door. There were things going on here that I would never understand, and with only a slight *frisson* of superstitious awe, I left them to it.

* * * * *

I drove into the parking lot of British Fish 'N Chips at exactly ten o'clock. Lester's red Jeep was already there, so I parked and went inside. He was sitting in a booth by the windows and waved at me.

"Nifty," I exclaimed, pointing to his khaki photographer's vest. Its dozen or so pockets were stuffed with pens, pencils, rolls of film, light meters — all the accoutrements of a photographer.

"I thought you might want some stills, too," he explained sheepishly. "So I needed to bring all my gear."

"Very resourceful of you," I told him. "Are you eating? Or are you starving that flu of yours?"

"No, I knew I'd be joining you so I had breakfast at home. Orange juice, eggs and bacon, toast and tea. You know — normal food."

"Why, Lester," I said, perusing the menu. "Could it be that I detect a note of criticism regarding my eating habits? What's wrong with fish for breakfast, anyhow? Think of all that Omega-Three fish oil — it's good for your heart." A cheerful young thing in a blue uniform appeared at my elbow. "I believe I'll have the Rock Cod Special," I told her. "With a double order of cole slaw. And coffee. Black."

Lester shuddered and shook his head. "Maybe just a cup of tea. I have the flu," he explained to the waitress.

"Normal food, eh?" I teased him. "Lester, how old-fashioned of you. I thought youths of today were more adventuresome. Daring, even."

He peered at me over the tops of his aviator glasses, blue eyes serious. "I can never tell when you're pulling my leg, Caitlin. I hope you're not —"

I patted his hand. "Consider it pulled."

He relaxed visibly. Sensitive soul that he was, how on earth would he ever make it as a journalist? I couldn't picture him in the thick of some hairy situation, asking unpopular questions. He worried far too much about what people thought.

"Let's talk a little business before breakfast comes," I said. "I don't want the rock cod to spoil your concentration."

"Okay."

"The place we're going is basically a laboratory

for a cosmetics company called Living World. They're supposed to be ethically responsible — that means they don't test their products on animals. So they say. But according to my client, Living World is fibbing." My breakfast arrived, and I decided to let Lester mull this over while I tackled the cod. It was flaky, moist, white, and delicious.

"So you want to find out where they're hiding the test animals, right?" Lester said after a few minutes.

"Right. And they won't be about to show us."

"What should we be looking for?"

"Locked doors, I guess. We'll encourage them to show us everything. Let's see what they leave out. We'll get shots of as much of the interior as we can — the exterior, too. Then when we're done, we're going to replay the tape and make a map. The animal lab will be somewhere inside that building. I'm hoping you'll help me figure out where."

"Sure," Lester said. "Then what?"

"Then what?" I wiped my fingers carefully with my napkin and took a swallow of coffee. "Then I get you to show me how to operate that video camera so I can go back there and get the evidence."

"You're going to break in," he said, his voice worried.

"Looks like I'll have to."

"Gee, Caitlin, er, I mean —" His eyes were eager.

"Whoa, boy," I told him. "The answer is no. Definitely and absolutely no." He seemed so crestfallen that I thought I ought to be more appreciative. "Don't think I'm not grateful for the moral support. Of course I am. But it's too dangerous, Lester. If we're caught, and they call the cops, you could kiss your career goodbye. But I have nothing to lose."

I didn't tell him the real reason, of course. I didn't believe for a minute that Living World would call the cops if they found me prowling the halls. Why should they, when they could whack me over the head and dump me and my car into the sea. Just as they'd done with Mary. Another traffic fatality. I was prepared to accept that risk for myself, but there was no way I was exposing Lester to it. I was ashamed of myself for even having considered taking him with me. "You'll have more than done your part today."

"Okay," he said reluctantly. "But remember, the offer's still open."

"I'll remember," I said, patting his arm. "Now let's go do that interview."

* * * * *

Living World was located in a clearing in the pines, down a narrow road off the Saanich Highway. We almost missed the sign bearing the distinctive Living World logo — two cupped hands cradling the cloudy blue globe of the earth — as it was partly obscured by a healthy growth of wild rhododendrons. We pulled into the parking lot at ten minutes to eleven, and Lester began unloading equipment from the Jeep. I got out, brushed some lint off my camel wool pants, and looked around.

From what I could tell, Living World seemed to be housed in an H-shaped one-story red brick building. The front of the building was one of the long sides of the H, and there was a small parking lot for visitors.

163

I noted with interest a sign that said EMPLOYEES and another that said DELIVERIES/PICKUP with arrows directing vehicles down an asphalt lane along the right of the building. I walked through the little parking lot until I could see down the lane. Just as I had thought, there was a guard in a hut, and a barricade operated by one of those electronic gizmos into which you slide a magnetic card. The hut sat on a little island in the middle of the asphalt, presumably so the guard could control traffic coming and going. There was certainly a lot of security for just an employees' parking lot, I thought. Yes, indeedy.

I walked back to the jeep and got my clipboard out of the back. On it I had actually written down some questions I wanted to ask.

Lester shouldered the videopack and the portable lights, and we walked up to the big glass doors and went in. He whistled. The lobby was about as big as a basketball court and paneled in rough-cut cedar, the ceiling at least twenty feet high. In the roof, half a dozen skylights directed the light onto a massive posterboard that was every bit of ten feet by six, hanging jut opposite the entry, where no one could possibly miss it. It depicted a wonderfully tanned, young blue-eyed blonde with long lustrous hair, white shirt open to the third button, smiling and holding out a big straw basket. In the basket were several unidentifiable green leafy plants, a paler green spiky leafed thing, a coconut, and a hunk of bark. I guessed these were supposed to be the ingredients of Living World's famous natural shampoo.

"Impressive," I said to Lester. "Can you shoot the poster?"

He put his gear on the floor, fiddled with the camera bag, and hefted the video camera up to his shoulder. "I'm not sure," he said. "The light isn't quite right, but I'll give it a try."

As the video camera clicked and whirred, I noted belatedly that far across the sea of dark green tweedy carpeted floor there was a small glass window in the wall. "I guess we hike over there to report in," I told Lester. "If I'd known, I'd have packed a lunch."

He put the video camera away, and shouldered his equipment again. "Ready."

As we crossed the carpet, I had the feeling that I was in some quiet forest glade. I felt calm and relaxed. Peaceful. Contemplative. You sap, I told myself as I realized what was happening. That's exactly what the interior decorator wants you to feel. Snap out of it. I decided to check out my impressions with Lester. "What does all this remind you of?"

He sighed. "Walking in the woods," he said dreamily. "I can even smell the cedar."

I sniffed. He was right. I eyed the cedar planks that lined the walls, willing to bet that some Living World lackey sanded them every couple of days to keep the cedar smell fresh. What a place.

We reached the glass window and I peered inside. A nicely groomed young man with expensively cut dark hair and a five-hundred-dollar navy blue suit sat at an oak desk, peering thoughtfully at the amber monitor of a computer. I knocked on the glass. He looked over, smiled brightly, and reached up to open the window.

"Can I help you? I'm Derek Angus, Public Relations."

I smiled brightly back. "I'm Caitlin Reece. My

165

cameraman is Lester Baines. We're from Channel Twenty-two. I believe we have an appointment with Mr. Maleck."

"Dr. Maleck," he corrected me.

Dr. Maleck, my eye. If the guy was a doctor, it was probably thanks to a purchased Ph.D. that had come in the mail from Fly-By-Night Tech.

"Reece, Reece," Angus said doubtfully, fingers busily clacking on the keyboard. "Oh yes," he said, "here we are. Oh dear — you mean they didn't tell you? And I called the studio myself." He looked at me speculatively. "You know, the young lady who answered the phone said that they'd never heard of you, but I told them they must be mistaken. After all, here you are." He gave me a tight little smile that let me know this game was up. Bright boy. He had called the station to double-check. And by some stroke of enormous bad luck, Lorraine Shaver must have been away from her desk at the time. Of course no one knew who I was.

I decided to bluff. "We're freelancers," I said coldly. "We don't *work* for Channel Twenty-two. We work for ourselves. What did you want the studio to tell us?"

"I'm really terribly sorry," he said, shaking his perfectly coiffed head in commiseration. "But it seems you've come all this way for nothing."

"Oh? Why, pray tell?"

"Dr. Maleck won't be available today for the interview. He was called away suddenly out of the province. A personal emergency," he confided.

A personal emergency? Hmmm. I wondered. Was Francis' electronic meddling setting up shock waves? Had Maleck left a pile of evidence somewhere that he was even now scurrying to bury? Very interesting indeed. Of course, he could have been speeding to the bedside of his ailing mother, but somehow I doubted it.

"Well, I'm terribly sorry, too," I said, adding an extra note of testiness to my voice. I really had wanted to get inside Living World once, legitimately. It would save me a whole lot of time if I could look around. But if I couldn't, I couldn't. "We've wasted a great deal of time coming out here," I informed Angus archly. "And time is money."

He said nothing, but showed us his dental work in a professional PR smile. Twerp.

"C'mon, Lester," I said. "Let's beat it."

* * * * *

"Now what?" Lester said as he let me out in my driveway.

"I guess I play it by ear," I told him. "I doubt we would have learned much, anyhow. So I'll just go in the back door and start there."

He swallowed, evidently unimpressed by my displayed sangfroid.

"Listen, kiddo, I've done this kind of thing a dozen times," I told him airily. "There's nothing to it. In fact, the most dangerous part of this whole operation may be the equipment."

"What do you mean?"

"Lester, I'm an electronic idiot. With my talent, I'll probably stick my finger someplace it doesn't belong and electrocute myself."

"No, you won't," he laughed. "It's really not hard at all. I'll show you everything you need to know."

167

"That's what I want to hear," I told him. "I'll call you Thursday around noon. I want to go in just after the employees leave. While I can still see without having to put lights on."

"Come on over," he said. "I'll be waiting for your call."

* * * * *

I changed clothes in my bedroom, putting my good pants and jacket back on their hangers. Then I paced, feeling more than a little panicked. Events were galloping away from me, and there seemed to be nothing I could do to rein them in. Dammit. I paced a little more, then decided to go get some therapy.

* * * * *

As I pushed open the heavy front door of The Shootist, the smell of cordite rushed to greet me. I'd forgotten just how pungent it was, and I rubbed my nose frantically, trying to ward off a sneeze.

I didn't recognize the man at the front counter, so I just showed him my gun club card and bought a silhouette target and my ammunition — a bag of one hundred .357 reloads. Through the bulletproof glass window across from the counter, I had already seen that there were only three other people practicing. I put on my ear protection and went on into the range. Muffled *craaks* attested to a .22 target pistol being fired; the steady, measured *booms* were undoubtedly from a .357, and the occasional cannon-like *blaam* was the distinctive sound of a .44 Magnum. I personally feel that not only is my Smith and Wesson

.357 Magnum sufficient firepower, but it's just about all I can handle. The kick from a .357 loaded with factory ammunition is about like the kick of a horse. But it's something you can learn to control. I'd fired friends' .45 automatics and .44 Magnum revolvers and decided that I'd have to lift weights to increase my arm strength if I wanted to shoot either of them. And lifting weights bores me.

I set my .357 in its carrying case down on the folding counter in front of me, hung my target on the clip over my head, and pressed a switch to send in downrange to the twenty-five foot mark. I always practice at this distance because I figure if I'm going to have to shoot anyone it will only be because he's coming at me with a deadly weapon and mayhem on his mind. And you sure can't tell that at any distance beyond twenty-five feet.

I hadn't done this for a while, so I recited the litany to myself. Load revolver, close chamber, take gun in two-handed grip, assume Weaver stance, align front and back sights with center of target, hold breath, and squeeeze. *Boom.* The gun kicked in my hand, but my tensed arm muscles controlled it. The sights were still steady on the bad guy's midsection. I squeezed again. *Boom.* For my third shot, I raised the muzzle so it pointed at the exact center of the head. Smoothly, I squeezed. *Boom.* Then I fired off two more shots to the body, and one to the head, put my gun down on the counter, and brought the target back in for inspection. Not too bad. My body shots were clustered in a grouping no bigger than a silver dollar, two inches to the left of the target's middle. I was up to my old tricks, letting my gun drift to the left. I'd have to hold it steadier. The two head shots were likewise off center, but I was pleased to note that the two shots had made only one hole. Nice. I took my packet of black target pasters out of my pocket, stuck them over the holes, and sent the target back downrange for a new sextet of shots.

As my ammunition dwindled, I improved. My shots were now grouped in the center. Of the body, and of the head.

"Two to the body to stop the bad guy, and one to the head if he's still coming for you," Brendan had taught us. "And what about the three shots you have left over? Do you pump them into him, too, just for good measure? Of course not! The three shots you have left over are for his buddy if he has one, or for him if he still won't go down. And don't worry about this nonsense of shooting to maim or shooting to kill. You shoot to stop. Period. You shoot because you believe you're in mortal danger. That's the only justification there is."

I emptied the last spent shells onto the floor of the range and packed my gun away in its carrying case. I'd have to clean it before I reloaded it, but that would have to wait until I was at home. Although I enjoyed coming to the range to practice, sitting around afterwards amid people with guns made me nervous. As I had hoped, the feeling of competence that shooting always brings, of mastery over this terrible, deadly force had had a salutary influence upon me. I felt confident and in control.

I don't understand the antipathy many women feel toward guns. I've been told it's a *political* thing, whatever that is, but I think that's a crock. Anyone can learn to use a gun — let's not kid ourselves about that. And anyone can learn the law — she can

170

educate herself about gun ownership and when the law allows you to shoot. No, women's reluctance to mess with guns is something else. All the symbolic crap aside, I often wonder if it doesn't come down to a question of nerve. Women just don't think they can do it. Beats the hell out of me why not. Maybe twenty years ago when we were all socialized into being passive as pussycats, but surely not today. Woman as victim is a tune that just won't play any more. But if we think we can sweetly reason the bad guys into leaving us alone, we're dreaming. For whatever reasons — testosterone, socialization, or just plain cussedness — men prey on women. And if you don't want to be victim, it seems only reasonable that you take some precautions. If you have something you value, you safeguard it. I have friends — perfectly reasonable people — who lock their houses, keep their gold coins in the safe deposit box, and get their flu shots regularly. But these same people aren't prepared to go to the wall to safeguard that most important asset of all — their lives. It just doesn't make any sense.

Of course, my line of work is a little different. I carry my .357 concealed illegally, but Canadian gun laws are among the toughest in the world and PIs get no special treatment. So I reluctantly break the law. I have no desire to meet again some of the bad guys I've bested in the past. I have no illusions that I'm more powerful than they are. Or that I ever could be. When faced with a sticky situation, my rule of thumb is to run. Quickly. In the other direction. If that fails — and it often has — I'll stand and fight. But I won't use the Marquis of Queensbury's rules. Are you kidding? I stand five-foot-eight and weigh in at 140. Most men I know could knock me into the middle of next week. No sirree. I need an edge. Something to persuade them to go away and leave me alone. And there's no more irresistible voice of reason than that of the .357. It's a wonderful mind-changer.

I let the door of The Shootist slam closed behind me. Gone was the mind-numbing, yammering panic I had felt when Lester and I returned from our aborted tour of Living World. I knew what I had to do — I'd known it all along. Now I just needed to bloody well go out and do it.

Chapter 13

I parked my car about half a mile down the highway from the Living World sign, and set off through the woods. My Reeboks made little sound on the carpet of pine needles, and here among the trees, out of the wind, it was quiet and peaceful. A lot like the lobby of Living World, I thought. Ahead, through the trees, I saw flashes of light — the sun glinting off chrome and windshields. I was directly behind the employees' parking lot.

As I had suspected, there was a fence. I tossed a pine cone at it, but nothing happened. Good. At least it wasn't electrified. Hands on my hips, I stood back and looked at it. It seemed to be your standard garden-variety cyclone fence — diamonds of sturdy metal wire just big enough to poke a sneakered toe into. I'd climbed dozens of them in my childhood. The difference with this one was that it was topped by three strands of barbed wire set about six inches apart. Goody. Well, never let it be said that I'm not resourceful.

I climbed the fence until my nose was level with the first strand of barbed wire, then hung by one hand and tossed the heavy six-foot tarpaulin I had brought with me onto the prickly points. I had doubled it, then doubled it again. I hoped that whatever protection it didn't offer, my battered leather jacket and Malcolm's heavy leather gardening gloves would provide. Tentatively, I reached up and hung one arm out over the tarp. Then I put my weight on it. So far so good. I put my other arm up onto the tarp; then, mindful of the sharp twists of metal only four layers of canvas away from my belly, I scrambled over the wire, hung from the other side of the fence for a moment, and dropped to the ground.

Okay, I said to myself, okay. Let's hit that parking lot, kid. Heart hammering, I sprinted across the asphalt and ducked down behind the first row of parked cars. No lemon yellow Buick. Crouching, I moved up one row. Nope. I started to sweat. The closer I got to the building, the greater my chance of discovery. It would be far too easy for someone to glance out a window and spot me. Still, there was nothing to do but go on.

I was halfway down the row just behind the

building when I spotted it. Actually it was a lemon yellow Oldsmobile Cutlass Ciera, license number BRY 801. Bingo. I duck-walked around to the passenger's side and whistled under my breath. The right front fender and the passenger door was scraped and dented in several places, dark red paint proclaiming the color of the car it had tangled with. Good. Mary evidently hadn't gone over the cliff without a fight.

I took the Polaroid out of my backpack, took a shot of the car that showed the license plate, one showing total right-side damage, and a closer shot of the fender. I scraped some of the dark red paint off the Cutlass into a plastic baggie, sealed it, and put it and the camera back into my pack, zipping it securely. Maybe Sandy could persuade someone that this was evidence. I certainly hoped so.

I had one last job to do, and I wasn't looking forward to it. I wiggled my arms through the straps of the pack, settled it securely on my back, and half stood, studying the back of the building. I wanted to find the doors. Directly in front of me was a wide set of four concrete steps. Those led to a set of double green metal doors conveniently marked EMPLOYEES ENTRANCE. Off to my left a ramp sloped down, leading to a roll-up overhead door marked DELIVERIES. The door was up, and a white van was pulled up at the loading dock. There was a small, unmarked door beside the delivery door, and I supposed this was where the truck or van drivers entered and exited while they waited to be loaded and unloaded. That looked promising.

Using the near row of cars for cover, I ran for the door beside the loading dock. I took off my backpack as I went, and tossed it up onto the closed lid of a dumpster that sat beside the door. All of a sudden, the loading bay door came down with a deafening clatter, almost scaring me witless. I hunkered down beside the dumpster, willing myself invisible.

"I thought they fixed this fucking thing!" a man yelled. "It's gonna take someone's head off. Pat, put a screwdriver in the gears!"

After a few moments, things calmed down. I raised my head, looked around, stood up, then walked to the door. Turning the doorknob, I pulled and to my surprise, it opened. Too late to turn back now, I told myself. I stepped inside.

Two men in heavy boots and green coveralls with Living World logos on the chest pockets sat in uncomfortable-looking chairs, drinking coffee and watching television. I almost laughed out loud. I'd walked into the blue-collar worker's lounge. One of the men — thin, young blond with a droopy moustache, looked guiltily at his watch, and got to his feet with such exaggerated nonchalance that I knew right away he had been goofing off. He opened his mouth to ask me a question, and I decided I'd better get the drop on him.

"Hey, have you seen A.J.?" I asked.

"Who?"

"The guy who came with me in the white van."

"Oh. I think he's getting his lading ticket signed," the blond said.

"Say, I haven't seen you here before." The other coffee drinker — an older, solid, dark-haired man — looked me up and down.

"The boss asked me to come along to keep an eye on A.J.," I invented. "We've had complaints."

"Oh yeah?" the dark-haired one said. "Like what?"

"He loses things," I said, rolling my eyes. "You know — he'll leave here with a dozen cartons, but when he gets to where he's going, there are only eleven."

"Nice racket," the blond said, looking at me and grinning. "So, are you going to be, you know, taking his place?"

I shrugged. "That's up to the boss. Say, is there a bathroom I can use?"

"Yeah," the blond said. "C'mon with me. This way."

I followed him out a door opposite the entrance and into a wide, well-lighted hall. We walked down it for about ten yards until we came to a T-junction. "Bathrooms are on your right on down the hall," he told me. "You can't miss them. I've got to go back to the salt mines," he said, leaning against the wall and grinning. "So what's your name?"

Ye gods, he was putting the make on me! Well, maybe he could be useful. I fluttered my eyelids. "Katie."

"Well, now, Katie," he said, "I hope you're not wasting your time with old A.J." Suddenly he wrinkled his forehead. "Funny, I thought his name was Gordon."

"Oh, it is," I said quickly. "A.J.'s just a nickname. We use it at the office. I guess I should call him Gordon in public."

The blond grinned. "Probably has some deep hidden meaning, right? Listen, I gotta go, but I wouldn't mind seeing you again. Do you ever go to the Dog and Pony?"

177

Not if I can help it, I thought. "Yeah, sometimes."

"Well, I'm usually there about nine every night," he said. "Just ask for Kevin."

"I might just do that," I told him. "Maybe even tonight. But right now, I gotta go too. Nature calls."

"You're a riot, Katie," he said. "So, maybe I'll see you tonight?"

"You never know," I told him. "Bye, Kevin."

He slouched off down the hall, whistling, and I fled to the bathroom. How long did I have before all hell broke loose? Only a few minutes, I figured. Good old Gordon aka A.J. would probably be back at his van by now. And once the other coffee-drinker started asking him about his partner, I'd be dead meat. Flinging open the bathroom door, I took a fast look under the cubicle doors and sighed with relief. I was alone.

In a flash, I was up on the counter, fiddling with the window catch. The window was hinged on the top and swung open easily. Thirty more seconds, I prayed, ripping a piece of duct tape off the roll I had stuffed inside my jacket. I taped the window catch open, made certain it would still fall closed, then levered myself up and threw a leg over the sill. Dropping to the ground outside, I looked back at the window. It certainly looked locked. Congratulating myself, I loped to the dumpster, collected my pack, and took off at a gallop for the rows of parked cars.

I had navigated my way to the row of cars nearest the fence when I heard it. The rhythmic *whock, whock* of feet running on asphalt. But these feet had toenails on them — I heard them clicking. There was no time to look, think, or even yell. I levitated onto the trunk, then onto the roof of the car directly in front of me. And not a moment too soon. I heard the scrabbling of nails on the trunk below and behind me. Crouched on hands and knees, I turned.

"Jesus!" I said. It was a Doberman, one of the red ones, fangs bared, front feet on the trunk, looking up at me and slavering. Great. Just great.

I have a healthy aversion to most dogs. My paranoia probably dates from the time I was attacked by our neighbor's German Shepherd at age five. But whatever its cause, my antipathy to dogs is powerful. I absolutely, positively don't trust them, and never put myself in a position where I have to depend on their good will. The only exception to this rule is Gray's Great Danes, but then, I consider them to be extensions of her. This Doberman, however, was not of that ilk. It was undoubtedly of the genus Guard Dog. And where there was a Guard Dog, there was probably a guard.

Why didn't it bark? I looked it in the eye and wondered how good my chances would be at administering a swift kick to its chops. It seemed to read my mind, gave a healthy "Rorf!" as if tuning its voice, then commenced to have canine hysterics. It rarfed and rorfed until I couldn't stand it any longer. In a minute it would have all of Living World out here, never mind the guard who was, I devoutly hoped, snoozing in front of his space heater, dreaming steamy dreams of the latest *Playboy* centerfold. But he wouldn't be snoozing for long. Not if Fang here kept up that awful racket.

"So shut up already," I told it, unzipping my backpack. I hadn't checked my Dog Dazer's batteries in ages, but I had confidence in the heavy-duty copper-tops I had put in last August. I hefted it, and aimed it straight at Fang's head. To my gratification, he acted as though a wasp had stung him. Shaking his head, he whuffed, sagged down from the trunk of the car, and still shaking, ran off in the other direction. I didn't wait to see any more.

I leaped off the trunk of the car. Plain old abject fear gave wings to my heels as I put my head down, pumped with my arms, and ran like hell. Evelyn Ashford couldn't have done any better. I knew there was no hope of hitting the fence at the spot where I had left the tarp — I'd already decided I'd be happy to hit it at all.

I looked up. The fence was fifteen yards way. Ten. Five. To hell with the last ten feet or so — I wanted to be airborne! I jumped — a leap Jackie Joyner Kersee would have been proud of — and swarmed up the mesh like an ape. I had one hand on the barbed wire when I felt something hit me just behind the knee. Something that bit.

"Aargh!" I yelled, kicking. One hand lost its grip on the wire as this heavy *something* pulled me down. I heard my jeans ripping, and suddenly I was free. Terror put my brain into neutral, freeing me from the necessity of thinking and the handicap of feeling pain. Instincts honed in the primordial ooze took over, sending me back up the fence like a gecko up a wall. "Oh shit, oh shit, oh shit," I gibbered as the Dobie jumped for me again, chomping down on my foot.

Fear gave me the strength of three ordinary women and I held onto the mesh this time. Then with one twisting lurch, I pulled my foot out of the

180

shoe and left it to Fang. Boy, did I have leverage now! I bent my leg, stuck my shoeless toes into the mesh, threw my arms up and over the barbed wire, and pushed off. I went over the top like a diver off the low board, like a pole vaulter clearing sixteen feet, like a penitent seeking heaven. There was only one thing wrong. I had to come back down. Off balance. Wrong end up, from a height of ten feet. Relax, I told myself, as I fell to earth. Think limp arms and legs. Think cat.

Whooof I heard myself say as I landed on my back. Almost simultaneously I heard a nasty *thunk* — exactly like the sound a ripe cantaloupe makes when it tumbles from the grocery bag onto your kitchen floor. Then I neither heard nor saw anything else.

* * * * *

Fang woke me. "Rorf, rorf, rrrorrARF!" he said, dancing like a mad thing on the other side of the fence. "GrrrARFARFARF!"

"Oh, shut up," I told him. I sat up and grabbed for my head. It was split in two, or maybe four. Worse yet, it rang, as though someone were beating the J. Arthur Rank movie gong somewhere behind my eyes.

"What is it, boy?" someone said, a voice that wasn't mine. Oh goody. The guard was coming. Now I could look forward to being shot as well as masticated.

I lurched to my hands and knees, hoped my head would stay on by itself, and staggered into the woods. I got about twenty yards before I fell into the pine needles. This is good, my inner voice taunted me as I lay on my side, looking at a line of ants marching up a dead leaf. Caitlin the Great Detective, lying here with her nose in the mud. There are dozens of people who would pay big money for this picture. Girl investigator gets her comeuppance. Well? Are you going to lie here and let them find you? I heard myself groan in reply. Yeah, I answered, I kinda thought I would. I'm feeling puny, if it's all the same to you. But that pain-in-the-ass inner voice continued. Oh no, you don't! Up and at 'em. On your feet. Once more unto the breach. Half a league, half a league, half a league onward! I groaned again and rolled to my knees. Okay. I'd try.

Some homing instinct I didn't know I possessed led me to my car. Fishing the keys out of my pocket, I put them in the ignition, and without taking off my backpack, pulled out onto the highway. McDonald's was about a mile farther on the right, and I drove there in first gear, the traffic honking and zooming past me. I parked near the back of the lot, and concentrating fiercely, took two quarters out of the change holder in my glove compartment. Very slowly, very carefully, I walked to the phone. But when I got there, I found that my mind was a blank page. I couldn't even remember my own phone number. I leaned my forehead against the cool metal of the booth and concentrated as hard as I could. It worked. Something came. I inserted the quarter with fingers that had begun to shake, and waited for the dial tone. Please be there, I whispered, knowing I had one shot at this.

"Hello," a voice said. Whose voice, I had no idea.

"Who's this?" I rasped.

"Alison," she said warily.

I started to giggle. Why, out of all the people I knew, did I call on her for help? "Don't hang up," I said quickly, trying to stifle my laughter. "It's Caitlin." I managed to tell her where I was, and I managed a fairly steady walk back to my car. I wrote a note on a piece of paper, jamming it in the zipper of my jacket where it would be sure to be seen. Then I passed out, falling down, down, into an oily black sea where there was neither sound nor light. I'm dead, I thought as the Leviathan that always waits in those terrible, lonely dark places reached eager hands to draw me deeper. Dead.

Chapter 14

Someone was shaking me. "Caitlin," a voice said urgently. "Caitlin! Come on, please wake up. Why won't she wake up?" the voice asked someone else.

"Oh, she'll wake up," another voice answered, a gravelly, curmudgeonly voice I knew well. But for the life of me, I couldn't put a name to it. And besides, I didn't want to wake up. I decided to ignore both voices.

I heard a muffled *craak,* then a pungent, acrid odor stabbed sharp fingers up my nose. "Gaaak!" I said, snapping my head smartly away from that revolting smell.

"A little ammonia does it every time," Emma Neely's voice said.

I opened my eyes. I was lying on my stomach, on an examining table in Emma's animal clinic. I still had on the turtleneck I had worn for my adventure at Living World, but judging by the draft swirling around my hindquarters, I figured I must be *sans* jeans. "I didn't know they made tables this big," I said grumpily.

"Ah, it lives," Emma said, bending over to look into my eyes. She shone a light in each of them, and grunted a little. "Not too good," she said. "You took an awful whack on the head. But that's nothing compared to your dog bites," she said cheerfully. "What was it — a Doberman?"

"Grrrr," I replied.

As if they had been waiting to be called upon, my bites began to hurt. First they twinged, then they settled into a good steady throb. I flexed my foot experimentally and was happy to note that though it was painful, I could still move and wiggle everything. Thank the Lord for my new leather Reeboks.

"Well, let's get on with this," Emma bent down to look me in the eye again. "Are you sure you don't want to go see a people doctor," she asked. "It seems to be just a suturing job, but human anatomy *is* a little out of my league."

"I'm sure." Maggie Kent, my friendly ask-no-questions physician, was out of the country for a few months. I'd been trying my best to stay out of trouble in that time, but alas, trouble had caught up with me. I figured Emma could handle it. After all, a suture is a suture, as Emma had so pithily remarked. "Just pretend I'm a pedigreed poodle with my show career ahead of me."

"Do you want me to leave?" a small voice asked.

Alison. I'd completely forgotten about her. "Wait a minute, Emma," I said quickly. I hitched around so I was lying on my side. Alison sat on a straight-backed chair against the wall, my leather jacket and jeans in her lap.

"I'll just go fetch a few things I'll need," Emma said discreetly, leaving us alone.

"Thank you for coming," I told Alison. "I'm sorry I had to drag you into all this, but yours was the only phone number I could remember."

She put my clothes down on the floor and came over beside me. "I'm already in all this," she said. "Remember?" Her eyes filled with tears. "My God, Caitlin, you could have been badly hurt."

"Yeah, well," I said sheepishly. "Next time I'll be more careful. Or run faster."

She brushed the hair out of my eyes. "I'll wait outside. I don't have a strong stomach for this sort of thing. Then will you come home with me?"

That was the best offer I'd had all day. "Sure," I told her.

She squeezed my arm and left.

I rolled back onto my stomach, put my head on my crossed arms, and prepared to suffer. The door opened and closed behind me.

"Now, you'll just feel a little sting," Emma said in that smarmy voice all doctors use when they're about to hurt you like hell.

"Ha," I said.

"Here we go," Emma said, stabbing me in the calf with a needle that felt about as dull as a butter knife and as long as a javelin.

I ground my teeth together and, after few initial moans, prepared to endure.

* * * * *

Alison helped me hobble out of her Toyota Camry and up the steps to her house. It's hard to summon up any dignity when you're minus one shoe and have one leg of your jeans slit up the seams. Emma had wrapped my bandaged foot in a plastic bag to keep it clean, and I hopped gingerly, leaning on Alison. I felt about eighty years old, but at least there was no pain. The shots Emma had given me had taken care of that. I couldn't believe that it was still the afternoon of the day Lester and I had gone to Living World. It felt as though months had passed.

She settled me in the living room with a footstool and a pillow under my right foot.

"I'm going to get one of my pairs of sweat pants," she said. "And some socks. Then you can get rid of those jeans, and that plastic bag. I might even be able to scare up some shoes that would fit you."

I wiggled my size-nine foot. "Really?"

"Yeah," she said, smiling. "Ian just bought some new sneakers. They're still in the box."

She went upstairs and I leaned back in the armchair, feeling worried, ill, and tired. Now what? The way I felt, I would certainly be out of commission for the rest of the day. That left only tomorrow for me to do something productive. Friday would be too late. I closed my eyes. Tomorrow was

Thursday, wasn't it? Yeah, it was. Okay, fine. Then tomorrow it would have to be. I closed my eyes.

"Caitlin!" Alison said in alarm. "I don't want to nag, but Emma said I wasn't supposed to let you sleep. Not until tonight, anyhow."

"Oh, yeah," I said groggily, recalling her instructions. Opening my eyes very wide, I tried to will myself awake.

"I found these for you," she said, offering me a pair of navy blue sweatpants. They looked a little short, but what the heck. Beggars couldn't be choosers. I unlaced my right shoe and took it off, then unwrapped my left foot, giving Alison the plastic bag. Standing up, I winced. The local anaesthetic was beginning to wear off. The puncture wounds on my ankle and the sutures on the back of my calf were beginning to protest. Alison came over and offered a shoulder. I leaned on her while I unzipped my jeans, let them fall, then stepped out of them. One hand on Alison's shoulder, one hand wrestling with the sweatpants, I finally managed to hop my way into them. As I suspected, they were short, but I was beyond caring. I put one of Alison's socks on over my bandaged left foot, then sat back down in the armchair, feeling as though I had just done a hard day's work.

"Brother," I said. "Maybe I'm getting old, but I have a renewed appreciation for the frailty of the flesh."

Alison sat on the arm of my chair. "Do you want something to eat?"

I considered this question. Did I? When had I last eaten? I decided it must have been the Rock Cod Special that morning. I didn't feel at all hungry, but maybe I should eat something. Just to keep my strength up. "Maybe something soupish," I said. "You know, chicken noodle. Something like that."

"Okay," Alison said. "I'll be in the kitchen for a while. Anything I can get you in the meantime?"

I looked around. "How about the telephone? And something to write on." I smiled at her, trying to project confidence. "Time to see how the battle is progressing on the other fronts."

She handed me the phone with a skeptical look, then went on into the kitchen. I didn't blame her. My confidence-projecting ability was at a low ebb.

Francis was unavailable, so I was unable to cross his name off my list. Darn. I had hoped he would have something for me by now.

Gray was next, and she answered her phone on the third ring.

"Hi," I said. "How are Repo and Jeoffrey getting along?"

"They're sleeping together in Jeoffrey's cage," Gray told me. "Repo evidently considers himself Jeoffrey's protector. He seems quite happy in the role. He has eaten both breakfast and lunch, is playful and alert, and has groomed himself extensively."

"Hmmf," I said. "He sounds like his old self. And all this fuss was because he wanted a kitten?"

"Apparently."

"There's no figuring cats," I told her. "Listen, I might have to leave Repo there a little while longer. Something's come up."

"Come for him whenever it's convenient," she said graciously.

"I appreciate it, Gray."

Lester didn't answer his phone, either, and I was

just about to give up when a breathless female voice said, "Hello?"

"Er, hello. Can I talk to Lester?"

"Oh, well, yes you can," the voice said, flustered. "Well, that is you could normally, but you can't right now. Lester's still at the hospital."

"Still *where?*"

"The hospital. He was in a car accident. They're setting his arm right now. He just called me for a ride. I live next door," she explained, "and I'm already late for work. Say, are you a friend of his?"

"Oh no," I whispered, a horrible premonition lifting the hairs on the back of my neck. "Oh no."

* * * * *

In the harsh light of the emergency ward, Lester looked about the way I felt. The right side of his face was scraped raw, there was dirt ground into his jeans, dried blood in his hair, and his right forearm was now encased in a white plaster cast.

"What does the other guy look like?" I asked him.

"Hi, Caitlin," he said in surprise. "Where's Dorothy?"

"I told her I'd come and get you," I said. "She had to rush off to work, anyhow. So tell me what happened."

"I dunno," he said, shrugging. "Some jerk tried to run me off the road."

My stomach fell into my borrowed shoes, and I swallowed. "A jerk in a yellow car?"

"Yeah. Hey, how did you know?"

"I'm psychic," I told him grimly. "Lester. Now

think back to this morning. You let me off in my driveway. Then what did you do?"

"Well, I had to go back to Living World."

"You *what?*" I said faintly.

"Went back to Living World. For one of my portable lights. I forgot I'd left it in a corner of the lobby."

I sat down heavily on the bed by his feet. "Did anything happen there?"

He shook his head, plainly mystified. "Like what?"

"Like anything, Lester. Think."

He wrinkled his brow. "Well that public relations guy — the one we met — made me wait a bit because they'd had a security breach. Had to call out the dogs, he said. But he gave me coffee and some magazines to read. A guard poked around in the jeep a little, then they let me go." He shrugged. "No big deal. Then, when I was halfway home, that nut case in the yellow car came out of nowhere and sideswiped me. I took my foot off the gas and steered for the shoulder. Lucky for me there was a nice shallow ditch. I flipped the jeep, but by then I was going pretty slow."

"Did you tell this to the police?"

"Yeah. Someone came and took a report."

"Did you get his name?"

Lester frowned. "Peters, Petrie. Something like that. Why?"

"I like to know these things," I told him. "So, are you ready to go?"

"Yeah. I was just waiting for Dorothy."

"C'mon, then."

"Ouch," he said, climbing down from the bed.

"What hurts?"

"What doesn't?" He hobbled a little way down the hall before he noticed that I was hobbling, too. "Say, what happened to you?"

"Me? Nothing much. Just an argument with a Doberman."

"Oh," he said, looking at me, eyes wide in sudden comprehension. "Caitlin. You weren't —"

"Don't ask," I told him.

"Right," he sighed.

Putting an arm around each other's waist, we shuffled like nonagenarians out into the late afternoon sunlight to where Alison waited in the car.

* * * * *

Alison pulled up in front of Lester's house — a white side-by-side duplex with an enormous holly hedge separating the yard from the sidewalk. He dragged himself out of the car, groaning, and stood on the sidewalk, his face so pale his freckles stood out like crumbs on a tablecloth.

I rolled down the window. "Go to bed, kiddo."

"There's something I forgot to tell you," he said weakly.

"What?"

"The video equipment. It's, well, it's wrecked."

"Oh, no."

"Yeah," he said, looking tragic. "When I rolled the jeep it fell out. The camera is a total loss."

I felt a little tragic myself. "How much?"

"About two thousand."

Now I felt sick. "Don't worry," I told him, feigning insouciance. "I'm good for it."

"But what about tomorrow night?" he asked, a worried frown on his face. "What will you do for equipment? Heck, you don't even know how to use it."

"Are you kidding?" I said breezily. "I'll just head for the local video shop. They'd be happy to set me up with something. And we'll let them do the teaching." I winked. "I'm a quick study. Don't worry, Lester. It'll all work out."

He sighed. "If you say so. The way I feel, I'd like to sleep for two days. But if you need me . . ."

"You take care of yourself, now," I told him. "I'll call you soon."

We drove down Foul Bay Road to the ocean in a ruddy sunset glow that promised good weather tomorrow. Red sky at night, sailors' delight. But for the life of me, I couldn't summon up a scintilla of optimism. I hurt everywhere, and pretty darned soon, Alison or no Alison, I wanted to lie down and have a good cry. It may not be very grown-up, but I've found it to be extremely beneficial.

"That was very nice," Alison told me, pulling into the driveway and shutting off the Toyota's engine. She turned to face me, the sunset behind her turning the sea to a sheet of amber. Her hair shone golden, her eyes glinted like pools of quicksilver. I had to remind myself to concentrate on what she was saying.

"What was nice?" I asked.

"The way you talked to Lester. You made it easy for him."

"Oh, that. Well, I owed it to him, didn't I? He

193

wouldn't be in such bad shape if it weren't for me. I got him into this."

"And I got you into it. Don't you think this is getting out of control? Maybe we should back off."

"Oh, I don't know," I said. "Things are getting a little hairy, that's all. I wouldn't exactly say they were out of control." I looked at her thoughtfully. "You're the boss, you know. Do you want me to quit?"

She closed her eyes. "I don't want anyone else to get hurt. And I'm afraid they will. I'm afraid you will."

"I might," I said honestly. "But surely you realized that when we started. The folks at Living World mean business. They ran Mary off the road. They just tried to do the same thing to Lester. I don't know about you, but I get mad when friends of mine get hurt. It kind of makes me want to get even. Taking a few lumps seems a small price to pay for putting those guys out of business." But, after all, the decision was hers to make. If she wanted me to quit, though, I needed to know about it pretty soon. My mind was already turning over the problems associated with hauling video equipment through Living World's bathroom window.

"I'd like to put them out of business, too," she said. "Of course I would. But . . ."

"But?"

She put a hand on my arm. "Just promise me you'll be careful. I'm afraid you're determined to be a hero."

"Nope, not me," I answered mechanically, my mind on her hand, not her words.

She squeezed my arm. "Please be serious."

"Okay, I'll be serious. Of course I'll be careful. Why wouldn't I be — after all, this is my hide we're talking about. I have a plan for tomorrow night. I know how to get in and how to get out." I thought of my .357, lying in its shoebox. "And I'm going to take a friend with me."

"You are?" she said hopefully. "Then you're not going in there alone after all! Caitlin, I'm so glad." She squeezed my arm. "Come inside, now. Emma said you were supposed to rest."

With the agility of a gazelle, she got out of the car and ran up the steps. When I figured she couldn't hear me, I moaned, unfolding my protesting limbs and limping after her, feeling as ponderous as a pachyderm.

I surveyed the four steps up to Alison's house with all the enthusiasm of a patient anticipating periodontal surgery. On the first step I decided my left calf from which Fang had nipped his pound of flesh hurt worse than anything I'd ever endured. On the second step I amended that decision — my right foot which he had mangled in an unsuccessful attempt to part it from my body surely hurt worse. On the third step my head began to pound as though someone were inside beating enthusiastically on a sheet of metal, and I decided *it* was unendurable.

"Coming?" Alison said brightly, sticking her head out the door to see what was taking me so long.

"Just enjoying the night air," I said just as brightly.

While Alison locked the front door, I navigated a none-too-steady path to the living room and sat down on the couch. Sitting felt so good I decided I'd lie, so I scooted down a little and got horizontal.

"Caitlin!" a voice called from very far away.

"No," I whimpered, refusing to open my eyes. "Not now. Please."

The voice fell silent. I felt ill, hurt, and hopeless. I wanted oblivion. Someplace dark and still. Someplace where no one could find me. I let sleep wash over me in a black, oily wave, and when it ebbed it took me with it, pulling me under. I went willingly.

* * * * *

"Caitlin," someone said, shaking me.

I swam up through layers of sleep, finally breaching the surface of consciousness, coming awake. "Mmmph," I grunted, opening an eye.

Alison sat on the floor by the couch, one hand in my hair, her face inches from mine. "Emma said you weren't to sleep too long at any one time," she said apologetically. "It's been two hours. And you never did have that soup."

I looked into her silver eyes and took a deep breath. Soup was not exactly what was on my mind at the moment. "Great idea," I lied, sitting up. Swinging my sore foot gingerly onto the floor, I put my weight on it and winced.

"Let me help," she said, standing up beside me. Slipping an arm around my waist, she looked up at me questioningly. "Okay?"

"Okay," I said, acutely conscious of her nearness. I must have telegraphed this to her in some way, because all of a sudden, she was in my arms.

"Caitlin," she said, putting both arms around my waist, pulling me close.

"You're taking advantage of my weakened

196

condition," I said shakily. "I'm drugged. I'm feeble. I'm *non compos mentis.*"

"Good," she said, laying a finger across my lips. "That might be the only way I'll get you into my bed."

I couldn't think of a good reply for this, so I bent down and kissed her. Once. "Listen," I said, "I want to know that you're . . . sure about this."

"Sure?" she asked fiercely, looking up at me. "Who can be sure about anything? All I know is that I want you to come upstairs. I want to hold you. I want you to hold me. Dammit, I want to go to bed with you. That's enough for me."

She was probably right — who could be sure about anything? And the fact that she wanted me, was, at that moment, good enough for me, too.

* * * * *

Upstairs, in the light of a little lamp with an amber shade, she pushed me gently onto the bed. "I know what you meant downstairs," she told me softly. "But I am sure. Very sure. I turned my back on Mary, and I'll always regret it. I don't want to do the same thing with you." She lay on the bed beside me, head propped on one hand, the other hand on my shoulder. "I've been attracted to you since that first afternoon at Victoria Jane's. And finally I asked myself why. Why shouldn't I want you? I've gotten into the habit of denying myself pleasure. Well, I'm tired of it."

And all along, I had been fighting *my* attraction for *her.* What irony. I raised one hand and put it behind her head. Under my fingers, her hair felt as fine and curly as a child's. "I'm tired of it, too," I told her. "Very tired."

I pulled her head to mine and kissed her gently on the lips. At least I began to kiss her gently. Alison, though, had other ideas. As our mouths met, she opened her lips under mine, touching my tongue tentatively once with hers, then drawing away. She buried her face on my shoulder, leaving me surprised, and more than a little confused. She wanted me but she didn't want me? What was going on? Suddenly, though, I understood. Cool Alison, calm Alison, in-control Alison wanted, *needed*, permission to be passionate. I put my fingers under her chin and lifted her face to mine. "It's all right," I told her. "You deserve this."

She looked at me in the amber light, eyes enormous, and I kissed her again. I was not quite so gentle this time, and as her mouth opened under my kiss, I noted how eagerly her tongue sought mine. I held her tightly against me, and when she moaned, deep in her throat, I felt my stomach clench in desire.

Running my hands over her back, I bent to kiss the soft skin of her throat, inhaling her, the scent that was Alison. She put her head back, hands in my hair, and I unfastened one shirt button after another, kissing an imaginary line that led from the hollow of her throat to the top of her jeans. With an inarticulate sound, she pushed me down on the bed and knelt over me, straddling my legs. I put my hands on her warm flesh, and she closed her eyes as I caressed her back, her ribs, her stomach. When I cupped the soft weight of her small breasts in my hands, rubbing my palms over the hard little nipples, she gasped.

"Oh, God," she said, panting a little, leaning forward. "I can't stand it." Quickly, fiercely, she fitted her mouth to mine, kissing me deeply, urgently. I unfastened the top of her jeans and pulled the zipper down as far as I could. She shivered, and as I brushed the skin of her stomach, my probing fingers finally reaching the crisply curling hair between her thighs, she cried out, rolling onto her back, pulling me atop her. She slipped a knee between my legs, then arched her body to mine, hands clutching my shoulders. "Caitlin," she said hoarsely, rubbing her body against mine. "I can't . . . wait much longer."

I pulled her shirt off and tossed it on the floor. Putting both hands inside her jeans, I peeled them off her and flung them after the shirt. As she slipped beneath the covers, I very cautiously took off my borrowed sweatpants, wincing as my hands brushed my wounds. Alison pulled my turtleneck over my head and held the blankets for me as I slipped into bed beside her.

She came into my arms like she belonged there, and I gasped at the almost electric shock I felt as her warm, naked body met mine. For just a moment, she let herself be held, then she moved against me, demanding, eager. I felt the wet warmth between her thighs as her legs gripped mine, and I rolled her over onto her back.

I kissed her mouth, her throat, her nipples, and trailed my lips down her body to her thighs, brushing the fine, curly hair in passing. She raised her hips to meet me, and I parted the fine hair, my tongue finding that hard little bud hidden like a pearl in an oyster. I kissed her silken folds, my tongue opening her like the petals of a flower, and she cried out, her hands in my hair.

"Don't . . . stop," she panted. My fingers slipped inside her and I began a rhythmic stroking. She cried out again, and I felt quick, strong spasms under my fingers as she tightened her hands in my hair, her body rigid. Then she relaxed, the spasms quieted, and I gathered her into my arms and held her.

"Caitlin," she said in a choked voice, turning her face up to mine. "Tell me everything will be all right. That it will all turn out. That no one else will get hurt."

I looked and saw tears on her eyelids, sparkling like diamonds in the lamplight. "Sshh," I told her, holding her close. "Everything will be fine."

She ran her hands over my arms. "You feel good," she said shakily. "Strong. Competent. I think I'll believe you."

I kissed the tears from her eyelids, and was about to tell her something else, something reassuring, something profound, but fatigue like a giant's fist scooped me up and crushed me, and I fell into darkness.

THURSDAY

Chapter 15

The smell of coffee woke me. Groggy, disoriented, I opened my eyes. Then I sat up in bed and panicked. Where was I? I recognized nothing. I felt as though I had been on a long and arduous journey and had returned to find that someone had redecorated in my absence. The mirror on the dresser showed me a tousle-haired, pale-faced apparition in a lavender pajama top. I fingered the flannel material in bewilderment, then, squinting, looked twice in the mirror to be sure it was me. Oh yeah, I said in relief to the reflection, I remember you. But where in hell are you and whose pajamas are these? Then it came back to me. Alison.

I rolled to the edge of the bed, then very slowly eased my legs over the side. Next I stood. Hmmm. Not too bad. I flexed, then took an experimental step. My wounds still hurt, but they were bearable.

I looked around for my clothes and found them folded neatly on a chair by the window. Recalling clearly how the clothes had been shed, I blushed. Sighing, I got dressed, went into the bathroom and splashed water on my face, combed my hair, then went downstairs. I found Alison in the kitchen, scrambling eggs.

"Hi," I said, feeling foolish.

Looking over her shoulder, she smiled. How could she make an old blue Chambray shirt and jeans look so terrific, I wondered. "Hi, yourself. Would you like to squeeze some oranges?"

"Sure."

"There's a bag of oranges in the fridge. The juicer is in the second drawer beside the stove."

I took the fruit, a knife, and the juicer and sat down at the big pine kitchen table. I was happy to have something to do. Morning afters are always so awkward.

"I called the towing company," Alison said. "They brought your car back from McDonald's about half an hour ago."

"Hey, thanks," I told her. As I juiced, I stole a furtive look at my watch. Good grief — it was almost noon! As though she read my mind, Alison spoke up.

"I know you have things to do," she said, "and if

you hadn't come downstairs by noon, I'd have gone to wake you. But I thought you needed your sleep. I checked with Emma and she said it was okay."

"Thanks," I said gratefully. "I do feel better."

Alison spooned the scrambled eggs onto two plates, added some fat slices of whole wheat toast, and brought the plates to the table. While I poured juice into two glasses, she got cutlery, a ceramic crock of butter from the fridge, and a glass container of jam. I suddenly realized I was starving.

She raised her glass of juice to her lips and looked at me across it. "Last night was very nice," she said. "You have no idea how nice. But I don't think this is the time to talk about it. Later, once this business with Living World is over . . ." She trailed off, looking miserable.

"Don't worry about it," I told her. "Neither of us made any promises. I understand."

"I hoped you would," she said. Then smiling brightly, she held her glass for a toast. "To success."

I clinked my glass against hers. "I'll drink to that. To success."

* * * * *

The Oak Bay Video Emporium was only too happy to rent me a nice, compact video camera and to give me a rudimentary course on how to operate it. Gwen, the store manager, took an impression of my VISA card as I fiddled with the camera. I figured the lighting would be as bad in the Living World lab as it was here in the video shop, but we seemed to be getting a fine picture. With a little practice, I found that I could even put the thing on my shoulder and hold it halfway still.

"We could set you up with a tripod," she suggested.

"No thanks," I demurred. "I'm going to be moving from place to place. Too much trouble." Besides, with my luck, I'd trip over the bloody thing, make a ferocious ruckus, and bring Fang slavering after me again. I chuckled, just thinking of him. Boy, did I have a treat for old Saber Tooth. "So how much will this be for, say, a day?"

"For this particular model — that'll be fifty-four dollars. Not including tax."

I winced. "Hey, I just want to rent the thing, not send it through school!"

"Well," she said huffily, "it *is* state-of-the-art. And you did say you wanted something that would record broadcast quality. Three-quarter-inch tape, you said."

"Yeah, yeah," I said ungraciously. "Okay. I'll take it."

"Fine," she said brightly. "Just have it back by tomorrow at five o'clock."

* * * * *

I let myself into my silent, cold house feeling about as low as I could recall having felt in a long time. I wandered around the living room, touching familiar objects, trying to make myself feel better, but it didn't work.

Some of my depression had its basis in fact — I was worried about how I would get this job done tonight. But the rest of my ennui seemed to have little to do with reality. Oh, I missed Repo, but he'd soon be home. I eased myself gently into my favorite armchair and decided I'd just sit there and brood. Maybe if I wallowed in the Slough of Despond for a while I'd get thoroughly sick of it. Like the time I ate too many caramels when I was nine and threw up my toenails. I couldn't eat a caramel today if my life depended on it. Maybe I'd try the Caramel Cure and OD on self-pity.

So all right, already, I said to my worries — do it to me. Report in. I closed my eyes and waited for the onslaught.

An image of Alison rose up out of my memory — my very recent memory — and I felt weak as I recalled the circumstances. Lamplight behind her made her hair the color of honey, and her eyes shone like silver coins. She bent over me . . . Enough, I told myself roughly. That was probably a once-only experience. Stop mooning over her. Right, I said obediently. I will. I sure will. Just as soon as my heart stops hurting.

I put my head back and stared at the ceiling. Caitlin, you're getting too old for this sort of thing, I told myself. All this adolescent swooning. The one night stands. Into and out of women's beds with the speed of light. You're probably getting a terrible reputation. I sighed. Dammit anyhow — I never wanted to behave like this. As corny as it sounds, I crave monogamy. I'd love to meet a woman with whom I could spend the rest of my life. Someone to go to movies with, to make popcorn with on winter nights, to plant flowers with in the spring. But the women I meet, the women I become involved with, are invariably unsuitable in some way. Either they're involved with other people, like Tonia, or just passing through, like Alison, or they turn out to be really not my type after all.

I've given this phenomenon of mismatching quite a lot of thought, and have concluded that the problem lies in the way I meet other women. Our liaisons just "happen." My God, we shop for coffee-makers more carefully than we shop for potential life partners. And the latter is surely a much more important investment because, unless you're particularly ruthless, you can't turf your new partner if the brew isn't as savory as you expected.

Okay, what else, I asked myself. Well, maybe Emma had put the thought into my head, but the way I made my living *was* beginning to get me down just a tad. Heck, I could see right now that I was never going to get more than a few thousand dollars ahead. Thank God I had bought my house — and had put a hefty chunk of change into the down payment — when I was still a real person. The rent I charged Malcolm and Yvonne covered my mortgage payment, so my real out-of-pocket living expenses were taxes, insurance, and maintenance. Whew. The rescuing, thwarting, and interdicting business just wasn't one of the world's better-paid professions. I gnawed a hangnail and pondered the implications of insolvency. What did it mean, anyhow? And did it matter? Well, it meant no expensive holidays. It meant no new car. It meant few luxuries. On the other hand, it meant no set hours, no time clock, no "have-tos," and no pressure save that of my own devising. It meant freedom, of a sort, and that mattered. And the intangible benefits — seeing good people happy again and knowing I did it — they mattered, too. I sighed. If things got really tough, I could always open up a law practice, I guessed. After all, that was what I had paid a whole lot of money to get trained to do.

The phone rang, interrupting my musings, and it was with a certain relief that I limped into the kitchen to answer it. Enough navel-gazing was enough.

"Home at last, I see," a fussy tenor voice said.

"Francis!" I exclaimed eagerly. "What have you got for me?"

"Quite a lot, actually."

I felt my optimism's Dow Jones rise a point or two. "Oh yeah? What?"

"You must be psychic, my dear. Your friend Evan Maleck aka Ivan Malecki aka Yvon Malik is, it appears, just a smidgen in arrears on his taxes."

I chortled. "Atta boy, Francis! How long is this smidgen?"

"Long," he said, snickering. "Very long. Nine years."

"All *right!*"

"And there's a certain James McLaughlin in the Ottawa office of investigations for Revenue Canada who has been working on the Yvon Malick case for quite some time now. I think it would be *marvy* if he were to hear about Mr. Maleck's alter egos, don't you think? Just an idea, mind you."

"It's always good to help the Revenue Canada folks. They're among my favorite people."

"Oooh, how catty you are. And you know, Mr. McLaughlin might also be fascinated by Living World's bank account. The business has a very creative tax attorney, so it legally pays no taxes, but its bank account shows a very substantial amount of money being paid monthly to Mr. Maleck."

"Money which Maleck doesn't declare. Tsk, how naughty of him. You're a genius, Francis."

"Yes, I am," he said without a trace of humility. "But that was so easy I decided to dig around for something else. After all, you have this petty bourgeois desire to get your money's worth. And this tidbit is even juicier."

"Oh yeah?"

"Maleck himself — not Living World — is in violation of a federal injunction. In nineteen-eighty, in Quebec, he was brought up on charges of mistreating his lab animals. The case caused quite a stir in the local papers, and the Superior Court found him guilty under federal law. Big deal. He paid a fine and that was the end of that. But because his animals had been obtained with money from a federal granting agency, he was prohibited from using any future funds he might obtain from that federal agency to buy lab animals."

"Francis, the suspense is killing me. Are you telling me that he just ignored this injunction?"

Francis cackled. "Exactly. Living World's Research and Development wing has been using federal money to buy lab animals for the past three years — as long as they've been operating in British Columbia. I have copies of their requisition forms and invoices. Right out of their own computers, I might add."

I was flabbergasted. "So he's been lying to everyone."

"So it would appear."

"This is terrific, Francis," I told him. "It's

dynamite. Just what I need. Can I come over and pick up the hard copies?"

"Any time," he said airily. "Always happy to please. By, dearie."

I hung up and began to pace, albeit a trifle limpingly. This information was wonderful. Much too wonderful to use for the petty blackmail I originally had in mind. No, it needed to be used in a much more formal way. I ran a hand through my hair. I knew what I wanted done — in my mind's eye, I could see the finished product — but who on earth could do it? Would do it? And do it in the next twenty-four hours, too?

* * * * *

"Let's go over this one more time," Lester said. "You want me to do the voice-over on a broadcast-quality videotape." He prodded the printouts of Maleck's financial data I had just gotten from Francis. "We'll include relevant financial information and super-impose it over the videotape of the animals at Living World. And we'll include stills — of Living World, of lab animals and so on." He looked at me over the tops of his glasses. "I don't think that'll be a problem. When can I have the tape?"

I crossed my fingers behind my back. "I'll probably have it later on tonight."

He shrugged. "Well, there's a do-it-yourself editing studio on Government Street. They open up at eight in the morning, so if I start as soon as I see the tape tonight, I can probably have a script written and ready to go by eight. Then, if you're not too fussy about quality —"

211

"I'm not. I just want it to be watchable."

"Okay, I could probably have a tape by, say, late afternoon. Is that okay?"

"Just." I looked in concern at his broken arm. "Can you do this job one-handed?"

"Sure," he said, holding up his left hand. "Fortunately, I broke the right one. I'm a southpaw."

"Good boy, Lester," I said. "I really appreciate this."

His eyes slid away from mine, and he straightened the papers on the coffee table, squaring up the edges with his long fingers. "Caitlin," he said, "I know you're up to something. Couldn't you level with me?" His Adam's apple bobbed once as he swallowed. "Is it that you don't trust me?" he asked quietly.

I sighed. "Look at me, Lester."

He did so, blue eyes earnest.

"I do trust you, kiddo. Believe me. But I don't want to pull you into this even more." I looked at his arm and felt sick. Hell, he'd already taken licks for me. "I need your help. But you can help without signing in blood. My problems don't have to be your problems."

He swallowed again. "If I knew more about them . . . I mean if you wanted to tell me more about them, maybe I wouldn't mind. Maybe I could really help. Another time, I mean." He held up his broken arm. "I'd be useless to you with this."

I felt touched. "I'll think about it," I told him. "No promises, hear. But I'll think about it."

He smiled uncertainly. "Do you mean that? You're not just putting me off?"

"I said I'll think about it. That's all I want to say right now."

"Okay," he said.

I ruffled his hair as I got up to go. "Thanks for your vote of confidence," I told him. "I'll bring the tape over as soon as I get it. Why don't you catch up on your rest in the meantime?"

He smiled up at me, looking like everyone's kid brother. "Okay."

Lester, Lester, I thought to myself, looking at his trusting blue eyes. I don't think I can. No matter how much you think you want to help me storm the barricades and carry the banner of truth and justice. Sorry, kiddo.

Chapter 16

I parked my car in the deserted lot of the Elk
Lake Boardsail Rental establishment, and hefted my
duffel bag full of goodies onto one shoulder. Setting
out through the woods, I quickly arrived at the
fenced-off back lot of the Living World employees'
parking lot. I crouched by the fence in the deepening
gloom, dismayed to see that two cars still remained in
the lot. One was a dark blue Cadillac, the other a
black Camaro. Damn it to hell. Well, what did I
expect? My unfortunate encounter with the dog
probably had security all atwitter. No doubt they

were battening down the hatches for an onslaught by rabid animal activists. Well, I'd just have to be careful.

I tossed my new tarp over the fence, climbed carefully, negotiated the barbed wire, and dropped to the ground on the other side. Kneeling, I tied a strip of fluorescent ribbon to the bottom of the fence. If I had to make a run for it, I wanted to be able to shine my light and hit the correct spot in the dark. I didn't intend to leave any more of my flesh at Living World.

Fishing the tranquilizer gun out of my duffel bag, I scurried across the parking lot, keeping a wary eye out for Fang. At the loading bay, I put my bag onto the dumpster, jumped up beside it, and reached up for the bathroom window. With any luck, no one would have checked. My tape ought to be still in place. It was. The window swung open smoothly. I propped it open, dropped the duffel bag through, then levered myself up with my arms, wriggling through the window to land on the lavatory counter. I reached up and pulled the window closed after me, then jumped down to the floor.

From the duffel bag I took the things I'd need, and laid them out on the counter. Video camera. Tranquilizer gun and lab coat provided by Emma. Magnetic lab pass, courtesy of Francis. Clipboard. And my .357 Magnum. I put my windbreaker into the duffel bag, and, clipping the .357 to the back of my jeans, slipped into the lab coat. I put the tranquilizer gun into one of the lab coat's pockets and the magnetic card into another. The video camera I put into a plastic contained labeled LAB CHOW. I kicked the duffel bag over into a corner, then, picking up the clipboard and the container, I realized with a little shiver of fright that I was ready. There were no more preparations to be made.

And I balked. I choked. Suddenly I didn't want to do it. I didn't want to go out there. My feet very sensibly refused to move. This was it — showtime, and I had stage fright. Jesus. I started to sweat. C'mon, c'mon, I urged myself. It'll be a cakewalk. But my feet, I noted, were still glued to the floor. Oh for heaven's sake, I told myself, go on. Stop thinking. Just get on out there and do it. So I did.

* * * * *

At the door just down the hall from the ladies' room, the one marked RESEARCH — AUTHORIZED PERSONNEL ONLY, I took the magnetic ID card out of my pocket and fed it into the metal box clamped to the door. With any luck, it would still work. Francis had done some fiddling with the card, and had assured me that the computer would recognize it as valid. When the green light on the top of the box glowed, I removed the card, and pushed the door open, silently thanking the talented little twerp. The door closed behind me with a *snack* of finality.

To my surprise, the doors lining this short hallway were all clearly labeled. I guess I had expected Living World to be ashamed of what they were doing and therefore to have the doors labeled with something cryptic. Nope. Halfway down the hall was a door marked TESTING. Bingo. I ignored the erratic cantering of my heart and pushed the door open.

The merciless fluorescent lighting illuminated a

scene I know I'll never be able to forget. Directly in front of me were about twenty animal cages. They were piled four deep on wheeled carts, so the topmost cage was just about eye level. I swallowed, and walked over to see. The cages were full. An albino rabbit raised its head from its dish of chow and looked at me, twitching its nose. I flinched, expecting the worst, but this rabbit seemed well. Its eyes looked absolutely normal. I checked the rabbit in the next cage and the next and found the same situation. Healthy bunnies. "Hi, guys," I whispered.

Belatedly checking for security cameras, I peered into each cage, making my way down the row. But at the last tier of cages, I stopped short. Here, the rabbits were not fine. Not fine at all. There were eight — two to a cage — and they all had wide, plastic cone-shaped collars fastened with snaps around their necks. They lay on their sides, in postures of despair. In places, their fur had been shaved to allow application of the test substance, and the naked, pink skin now bore angry red, suppurating sores. And their eyes. My God.

After one look, I sat down on the floor, wondering how I was going to do this. The whites of their eyes were crimson, so badly ulcerated that pus had oozed down onto their cheeks, staining their snowy fur green and yellow. Clearly the latest shampoo test had been a terrific success. I felt like throwing up. In one cage both rabbits were clearly dead, and in another they moved so feebly and so erratically that I had no doubt that they were dying. Why the hell hadn't they been euthanized?

I put my head down between my knees, took a couple of deep breaths, and got a grip on myself.

Standing up, I put my LAB CHOW container on a bench behind me, and took out the video camera. Taking another deep breath, I opened one of the cages. The rabbits, unable to see me, nevertheless heard the cage door opening and, scrambling feebly, moved as far away from it as they could. They recognized the sounds that preceded pain.

"Sorry," I told them, biting my lip, turning the camera's built-in light on them. I videotaped the inhabitants of each cage, included shots of the experiment protocol clipped to the cage doors, then turned the camera off.

I looked at my watch. I had been in here for twenty-three minutes, and it had all been too easy. It was definitely time to go.

I retraced my steps without incident, and it wasn't until I stood on the counter in the ladies' room, preparing to toss my duffel bag back out the window that it hit me. I couldn't leave the healthy rabbits behind. I just couldn't do it.

Closing my eyes, I leaned my head against the cool tile wall and tried to think. How was I going to take twelve lively rabbits to safety? I certainly wasn't going to be able to stuff them in my duffel bag and toss them over the fence. But speaking of the duffel bag, and the videotape, I had the strongest feeling that I ought to toss *them* over the fence to safety. As soon as possible. Immediately, in fact.

Okay, okay, I said to the voice nagging me to take action. I'll do it. One extra sprint to the fence and back — why not? The parking lot was empty now. With a sigh, I heaved myself out of the ladies' room window.

* * * * *

"Okay, guys," I whispered to the rabbits, back in the TESTING lab. "This is what we're gonna do. And it'll be a breeze." I found some wire, lashed the two tiers of cages together, and wheeled the whole thing toward the door. It would, I saw, just go through. On my way back from flinging the duffel bag to safety, I had ascertained that the roll-up loading bay door could be opened with my magnetic card without disturbing the alarm system. It now stood open six feet, waiting for me and my furry charges to wheel on through. I intended to pack them three to a cage, haul the cages over the fence, retrieve the duffel bag, schlep everything to my car, pack it all in and drive like hell.

Wiping my sweaty palms on my jeans, I opened the lab door and looked down the hall. No one in sight. Great. Propping the door open with my foot, I wheeled my load into the hall, one squeaky wheel doing a nagging solo.

"Hold it right there," a voice called from behind me.

Okay, Caitlin, this is it, I told myself. On stage. Time to bluff. "I beg your pardon," I said, turning around.

A bearded, exquisitely groomed, dark-haired man regarded me. Maleck, I was willing to bet. Shit! Why hadn't I checked the offices? I could have done that from outside — simply looked to see which lights were burning. Sometimes my lapses in logic amaze even me. Well, it was too late now.

"Where *do* you think you're taking those

animals?" he asked. Then, peering at me more closely, he inquired, "And who are you? I haven't seen you in the lab before."

I smiled what I hoped was a disarming smile. "Personnel just hired me on Monday," I told him. "And the lab supervisor left instructions for me to take these animals to the loading dock tonight."

"Oh?" he said, stroking his beard and looking at me doubtfully. "Let's see your instructions," he demanded, holding out his hand.

I sighed. So this wasn't going to be so easy after all. "Okay," I said, reaching into the pocket of my lab coat. I brought the tranquilizer gun up and while he watched, eyes wide in surprise, I shot him in the shoulder. He opened and closed his mouth several times, looking distinctly like a fish drowning in air. Then, taking two steps backwards, he collapsed bonelessly against the wall. Finally, he oozed down the bricks and just sat there looking up at me glassily. "Sorry," I said. "But you *did* ask."

I turned him around by his shirt collar, got hold of him under the armpits, and dragged him down the hall to the first unlocked door. STORAGE, it said. I checked his ID, and sure enough, it read Evan Maleck. Then I deposited him there on the floor, loosened his tie, made certain he was breathing all right, and closed the door.

"Come on, bunnies, let's make tracks," I muttered, sprinting back to my little prisoners. I had a bit of trouble negotiating the magnetic door, and a little more trouble maneuvering my way down the three steps leading to Shipping & Receiving, but finally we were there. The loading bay door was just

220

ahead. I permitted myself a tiny bit of optimism. We were going to make it after all.

Something hit me in the back, with enough force to knock me off my feet. I stumbled forward into the cart, and in another second I was on the ground, cages tumbling around my ears. As I frantically tried to get my feet underneath me, someone grabbed my hair and yanked my head backward. At the same time, I felt a needle being plunged none too gently into my neck.

"Have some of your own medicine, bitch," a voice said. Maleck's voice. "You really ought to have made sure of the dosage before you shot me."

"Silly me," I tried to say, but my tongue wouldn't form the words. It was just too much trouble. With a sigh, I gave up the struggle, and tumbled into oblivion.

* * * * *

I awoke behind bars. I was lying on my side in the testing lab, in a cage. I tried to get my hand underneath me to push myself upright, but realized with horror that they were bound securely behind my back. Great. Just great. I raised my head and looked cautiously around. The lab seemed empty, but I noted with a pang of sorrow that someone had transported the rabbits back here. I wriggled around and managed to sit up. Sort of. The cage in which I had been placed was probably meant for a large dog. It was none too roomy.

"Ah, returned from your chemically induced nap, I see," a voice said.

221

I didn't have to turn my head and look. I knew it was Maleck. But I looked anyhow. He was behind me, and it always makes me nervous when I can't see my adversary. As I turned, the unmistakable odor of gasoline filled my nose. Maleck was busy sloshing gas out of a metal container onto walls, counters, cages, filing cabinets, storage bins. He came over to stand in from of me and as I leaned back to look at him, the reassuring bulk of my .357 dug into my spine. He hadn't found it when he tied my hands! I guess he thought one gun — the tranquilizer gun — was quite enough for a lady to carry.

"What are you doing?" I asked him, although I knew perfectly well what he was doing. He was preparing to burn the place down. Destroy the evidence. And what — blame it on the Ninth Lifers? I wouldn't put it past him.

"Cutting my losses," he said, looking down at me, smiling a self-satisfied smirk. "You Ninth Lifers have caused me quite enough trouble. So I've decided to turn the tables. This little accident will generate so much sympathy for me in the community, and so much animosity for you, that you'll never recover." He chuckled. "And, of course, once we re-open for business across town, we'll announce a tour of our new facilities. There won't be a testing lab in sight."

"I can't believe you've had a change of heart," I said acerbically. "I'm sure you don't have one."

"Tut, tut," he said, sloshing a stream of gasoline in my direction. I bent my head and it hit me on the back. "It's politics, dear girl. One has to change with the times."

"Come on, Maleck," I said, twisting my hands inside my fetters. Plastic handcuffs, I decided. Not too tight, either. If I just didn't pull on them, maybe I could wriggle free. The gasoline helped. It trickled down the back of my lab coat and dripped onto my hands. I twisted some more. "How will you blame this on Ninth Life?" I asked, wanting to keep him talking. "There'll be no proof."

"Oh, won't there?" he asked. "What about these?" He reached behind the lab counter and emptied the contents of a sack onto the counter. For one moment, I thought he had my duffel bag, and my heart almost stopped. But no. The bag he held was an old Army-issue knapsack. I looked at the objects on the counter. A can of spray paint, some Ninth Life posters, a roll of tape. "These will be found in your car," he told me. "I'm sure it's around here somewhere. Parked in a desolate spot by the highway, presumably. I'll find it, though. After all, I have all night."

"Clever," I told him, twisting my hands. "But you've forgotten one important thing."

"Oh?"

"It's going to be obvious that the fire was intentionally set. How can I have done it if my body is found here in the cage?"

He tut-tutted again. "But it won't be," he said. "In a minute I'm going to give you another shot of tranquilizer. From your own gun, too. Not too much — just enough to render you harmless. Then I'll take the handcuffs off and leave you. You'll come around in a few minutes and it'll only take you a minute more to figure out how to get out of the cage. You'll be in a dreadful hurry, you see, because the lab will be in flames by then. You'll rush to the door," he said, clearly enjoying all this, "seize the handle and pull, only to discover that I've locked you in." He placed a hand over his heart. "How tragic." He looked at me levelly. "And whether you perish of smoke inhalation or die in the flames is really of no matter to me. I'll be rid of Ninth Life once and for all. Don't worry, my dear, I've thought of everything."

"Not quite," I said, as one hand came free. I bunched up the lab coat and drew my .357, aiming it with two hands squarely at his chest.

He blinked once, then, quick as a cat, he jumped behind the lab counter.

"Shit!" I screamed, banging on the locked door of the cage with my feet. The lock held.

I heard him chuckle at the same time I smelled the smoke. "Maleck, no!" I yelled. "No one will believe I set the fire!"

I guessed he didn't care anymore because from the other side of the lab counter came a dull *whoomp* and a ball of smoky orange flame. "Try hard," he said. "You can get out of that cage if you really want to." Through the smoke, I saw the lab door open, then close. The creep had gotten away. And he'd left me here to die. Just like the other animals who'd served their purposes.

"You bastard!" I screamed, kicking at the cage door. *No good, Caitlin, no good,* a little voice of calm told me. *Maleck might be right, but kicking the door off will take too long. Then you really will die of smoke inhalation. Shoot the bloody thing off.*

Of course. I put the muzzle of the .357 against the lock, put my forearm over my eyes and pulled the trigger. There was an ear-splitting *boom*, then, with a clatter, the cage door swung open.

I scrambled out, mindful of the fire which was just now spreading from the counter, finding the errant trails of gasoline, touching them with greedy orange fingers. The thought of my combustible lab coat didn't exactly cheer me, so I pulled it off and tossed it away. I figured I had only moments. I was right.

With another *whoomp,* the floor caught fire. The flames were now between me and the door, and I knew better than to hesitate. Shielding my eyes, I jumped into the fire. I was at the lab door in an instant, turning the handle, trying to push it open. But Maleck was right. He *had* locked it.

I coughed, choked, and figured I had about ten seconds to do something. Putting the muzzle of my .357 against the door just above the handle, I pulled the trigger twice. Through the thickening smoke, I saw that I had blown a hole the size of a tangerine in the door. Kicking the door, I noted it swung obligingly open. I was in mid-stride when I remembered them. The rabbits.

This time I didn't think. I didn't want to. Because if I did, I knew I'd never have the nerve to do it. Instead, I jammed my gun into its holster and ran back into the inferno. The flames had only just reached the animal cages, and finding nothing to burn, had started to blacken the metal on the wheeled cart. The rabbits were hopping around in the cages, trying to get away from this terrible, hot smoky *thing.* That's when it hit me.

The dream I'd had. The alien consciousness I'd inhabited for those few dream moments, when I watched in helpless terror as a great, red, glowing thing loomed toward me out of the gloom. I felt a moment of disorientation as something in my brain slipped a cog; then, with a spurt of horror I realized I was seeing the fire from the point of view of the caged animals, too. I was in their heads as well as my own. And their terror was paralyzing me.

"No!" I yelled, and something — the sound of my own voice, the heat of the fire, the shot of adrenaline I got from the terror of it all — canceled my mental double vision. I was now only Caitlin again. And I was about to be burned alive.

The smoke was choking me. Throat raspy with the need to cough, I made a grab for the cages and as my hands touched the metal, I screamed aloud. The smooth side of the wheeled cart was so hot I felt as though I had put both hands on the burners of an electric stove. I let go immediately, put my hands under my armpits and, eyes tearing with pain, booted the cart across the room with my feet. As I shoved it through the open doorway, I kicked the door closed behind me and collapsed against the wall.

Gasping, coughing, I allowed myself the luxury of looking at my burned palms and howling with pain. Then I shoved my hands back up under my armpits and nudged the cart down the hall with my feet. But it wouldn't move in a straight line. That bloody squeaky wheel had become locked in the heat, and now refused to roll at all. There was no help for it. I would have to push the cart. I wiped my tears on the arm of my turtleneck, put my pain somewhere else, and grabbed the cart.

"Let me help," someone said from behind me.

I felt I must be hallucinating, because when I looked back Judith Hadley stood there. Face pale and grim, dark shirt, dark clothes, dark gloves: she looked like a commando.

"Why . . . what —" I croaked.

"Never mind now," she said tersely. "All you need to know is that I'm here to help you. Alison told me what you were up to. And I knew I had to do this to . . . atone."

None of this made any sense, so I decided that I *was* hallucinating. Still, if the apparition wanted to atone . . .

"Help me push this thing," I rasped.

"Oh, God," Judith said, noticing my hands. "I'll push. You go open the door."

I took her at her word and ran ahead to the door with the magnetic lock. Suddenly I remembered — Mary's card was in the pocket of my lab coat. Then two things happened at once — the window blew out of the testing lab door sending fire spilling in both directions down the hall, and the lights went out.

"No power," Judith yelled. "We'll never get that door open now."

"Oh yes we will," I said grimly. Biting my lip to keep from crying out, I drew my .357. What the hell — it had worked once. Why not again? The fire behind us was the only light I had but it was enough. Blowing the lock off took two shots, but finally the door swung open, and we ran through. As I reholstered my gun, I thought: only one left. I remember feeling grateful to Judith that she hadn't tried to argue me out of bringing the rabbits with us, because I wouldn't have left them. They had become very important to me.

Finally, the loading bay door loomed just ahead.

Evidently Maleck had tried to close it and the bloody thing jammed because it stood open about four feet, a gray rectangle of night sky showing beneath it. But even though it meant freedom, it was about as inviting as the maw of a beast. I remembered how it had come crashing down the other day. Come on, come on, I told myself. It's locked open now. No power, remember. It can't get you.

"We're almost there," I said to Judith. "I'll go through first. Shove the cart after me when I'm out. Then you come on through and we'll push the rabbits up the ramp."

"Okay," she panted.

I rolled underneath the door, hitting my shoulder a painful thwack, and stood up. Breathing one lungful of cool night air, I looked up gratefully at the moon. By its light, I saw the cart come rolling out toward me. I grabbed it, and some superstitious dread made me pull it a couple feet clear of the door. Then I saw Judith's head and shoulders appear as she scuttled through the door on hands and knees.

"Be care —" I started to say.

The unthinkable happened then. With a rattle of chains and gears, the door fell. Judith looked up at me, and in the preternatural slowness that exists only in accidents or dreams, I saw realization in her eyes. And I saw something else, too. A kind of welcome.

Then real time kicked in, and I staggered forward to help, to pull her through, but it was too late. With one last hellish rattle, the door hit the concrete floor. There was one horrible scream from Judith, and then there was nothing else.

Chapter 17

"Judith!" I yelled, hauling at her shoulders. It was no use. The door had caught her just above the knees. All my pulling and tugging wasn't budging her an inch. She was trapped. I sat down heavily on the cold concrete, looked at the rabbits in their cages, at the pale oval of Judith's face, and closed my eyes tightly, hoping desperately that this was a nightmare.

"Caitlin," she said thickly.

I opened my eyes. It was no nightmare. Or, if it was, it was one in which I, too, was trapped. I rose to my knees.

"Go away," she said. "Go on. Get help."

"I —"

"You're no good to me here," she said, panting. "Go. Please."

"Why did you come here?" I asked angrily. "Why didn't you stay the hell away?"

"Like I said," she told me, biting her lip, "to atone. To help you. To make things right."

"To atone for what?"

She looked at me blankly. "For turning Mary in to Living World."

The words made no sense. "For —"

She shook her head at my impatience. "I did it. I told Living World that Mary was a Ninth Lifer." She smiled crookedly. "I didn't think they'd do anything to her — just boot her out. I wanted her great brave mission to fail. I wanted her to be . . . humbled in Alison's eyes." She began to cry then. "It backfired. It all turned to shit. Alison's been blaming herself, thinking that Mary's death was her fault. It wasn't. It was mine. I did it because I was jealous."

I felt like weeping. The always anonymous beast again. Jealousy.

"Go on," she said roughly. "And get these damned rabbits out of here, too. I'll be all right. Just hurry."

I decided I'd wheel the rabbits up the ramp, across the parking lot, and leave them over by the fence. Then I'd see if I could get back in the bathroom window. Judith needed help *now*. I'd come around to the loading bay and find some way to release the door from the inside. Feeling dizzy from the pain in my hands, the effects of Maleck's tranquilizer, and plain old fear, it took me much

230

longer than I believed possible to get the rabbits to safety. At the fence, when I turned to run back, I saw with dismay that the fire had burned through the roof of the south end of the building, and was now visible through every window. Mouth dry, I ran up the steps to the dumpster, leaped on top of it, and brought my head up to the level of the bathroom window. It was no good. The fire had already spread to the hall outside the bathroom. As I watched, the wooden bathroom door burst into flame, and the fire came roaring in like a live thing. I ducked, and flames shot over my head out the window.

I jumped down from the dumpster and raced back to Judith. "It's no good," I panted. "I can't get back in. I won't leave you here. The Saanich Fire Department ought to be here any minute."

"Caitlin," she said, panic in her voice. "The fire. I can feel it. My feet are hot."

"Oh, no," I whispered, and put my forearm on the loading bay door. I could feel it, too.

"Your gun," she said, beginning to weep. "Let me have it."

"My gun?" I inquired stupidly.

She clutched my arm. "Your *gun!* Give it to me, for God's sake. Or shoot me yourself. No one deserves to die like this."

Numbly, I handed her the gun.

The little door beside the loading bay burst open, and Maleck staggered through, clothes smoking. Either the power outage, or last-minute activities of his own, had trapped him inside the building. He choked, coughed, then vomited onto the concrete. When he straightened up, he saw us.

Then I did one of the hardest things I've ever

done. I begged. "She's trapped," I pleaded. "Come back with me. Help me pry the door up."

Eyes red-rimmed, clothes singed, he looked at us without a trace of compassion. "Why?" he asked. "One dead activist is as good as another." Then he turned his back on us.

Something snapped inside me then, and with a howl of rage, I took a dozen running steps and tackled him. We sprawled together on the asphalt of the parking lot, he struggling to escape, me relentlessly hanging on. He hit me on the side of the head with a roundhouse punch, and all the strength went out of my arms. He rose to hands and knees, looked at me, and stood up, a feral smile on his face. "Well, now," he said, reaching inside his jacket. "Why settle for one dead activist when you can have two?"

My .357 *boomed* then, and for one crazy moment, I thought Judith had shot Maleck. He turned, seemed to realize what had happened, then focused his attention on me again. I'm not certain what he was planning, because the world exploded then. I thought I saw an immense fiery shape — a creature with the body of an animal, eyes like the fires of Hell, and wings of terrible hot flame — erupt from one of the windows like a firedrake and swoop across the parking lot, picking Maleck up in its talons, immolating him instantly. But of course, I must have been mistaken. The exploded world began to fall on me then — hot, sharp, hurtful pieces of it — and I rolled myself up in a ball, waiting as dumb as any beast for the end.

SATURDAY

Chapter 18

"You're lucky you were on the ground," Lester said, handing me a glass of water and putting two painkillers on my tongue. "Maleck was fried when the windows blew out." He shuddered. "I saw it as I was driving into the parking lot. It was just like a flame thrower." I folded my gauze-mittened hands around the glass, bringing it to my lips and washing the painkiller down my gullet.

"Lucky is my middle name," I quipped, handing him back the glass. But somehow, my patter had deserted me. I had nary a wisecrack left in me. I felt

. . . empty. Hell, I'd done a terrific job — I hadn't gotten the videotape to Lester on time, the news had aired without us, CLAW was now holding a Day of Shame vigil in front of the burned shell of Living World — getting loads of good publicity out of that obscene act — and Judith would be buried Monday. Mary, Judith, and Maleck — all dead. Alison and Ian were back in Ottawa, conferring with their Ninth LIfe colleagues about how to proceed. Alison had paid my bill, including replacement by Ninth Life of the video equipment lost in the wreck of Lester's car. And I was flat on my back, with third-degree burns on my hands.

Well, not exactly flat. As the result of Lester's visit, I had emerged from my bedroom. I had even changed my sweats-cum-pajamas in honor of his arrival. After all, I reasoned, one couldn't entertain a gentleman caller in sweats which hadn't been off one's body for two days, now could one?

"You sound so . . . down," Lester said.

"I feel down," I said bleakly. "I wish I didn't. What did the Bard say: 'I have of late, but wherefore I know not, lost all my mirth'? Well, I know 'wherefore.' I botched things up, kiddo. I bungled. I dropped the ball."

"No you didn't," he said loyally. "No one could blame you for anything."

I put my head back and waited for the painkiller to work. "I do," I told him. "I do."

And this wasn't just self-indulgent whining, either. I really *did* blame myself. If I'd only been able to shoot Maleck before he set the fire, that horrible

236

conflagration could have been avoided. I wouldn't be burned, Ninth Life's "evidence" wouldn't have gone up in smoke, and Judith wouldn't be dead. Dammit, I couldn't be sure if I had taken that split second to correct my aim, or if I'd choked. Maybe I was getting too old for all this rough stuff. True, Val had the videotape, which the station intended to air legally on Sunday along with footage of the fire and a retrospective of Living World, but somehow I didn't much care. I shook my head. In the end I *had* done what Alison wanted. Living World was certainly out of business and Metro was re-opening the Mary Shepard case. But those facts were cold comfort. I still blamed myself.

"Want some supper?" Lester asked. "Yvonne left a casserole thingy in the fridge."

I considered with epicurean dread what might be lurking in the depths of Yvonne's casserole thingy, and decided against it. But I was getting a little hungry. "There's a microwave dinner in the freezer," I told him. "Shrimp something-or-other. But there's only one." Just in time, I remembered that I had been saving it for someone special. "What the heck," I said, throwing caution to the wind. "Let's do something really decadent. Let's order a pizza."

Lester beamed, and hurried over to the phone. "How about a medium with everything?" he called as he was looking up the phone number.

"Fine with me. Just hold the anchovies," I told him.

As Lester was dialing, a discreet tapping sounded on the door. Now what, I wondered. Getting up dispiritedly, I padded into the front hall, lifted the little curtain and peered out into the night. The caller was Gray.

"Well, hi," I said, opening the door. "What brings you into civilization?"

She smiled, then pointed behind her. Repo and Jeoffrey came strolling up my walk, Jeoffrey pressed close to Repo's side. As I watched, Repo climbed the steps very deliberately, Jeoffrey following him.

"Nyap," Repo said, rubbing his head once on my ankle before leading Jeoffrey into the house. I swallowed, a lump in my throat.

"Can he see *anything?*" I asked Gray.

"Some," she said. "He can distinguish shapes, I think, and day from night. Oh, while he's finding his way around, don't move the furniture."

"C'mon in," I invited. "Lester and I are going to have a pizza."

She shook her head. "No. But thank you anyway. I have to get back to work. A client is bringing her pony." She looked critically at my bandaged hands. "Was it worth the pain?"

I considered this. From anyone else, the remark would have been a criticism, but from Gray it was an honest question. So I answered her honestly. "I don't know," I said. "I never know. Results are important to the people who hire me, so I guess only my employer can answer that." I flexed my fingers inside the gauze. "But was it worth it to me? Yeah, it was. Not the outcome, but the effort. That's the most important thing — trying to keep the predators at bay. And giving it my best shot."

She smiled, nodded as though this made perfect sense to her, then walked away into the night.

I closed the door thoughtfully, feeling better than I had in two days.

In the kitchen, Repo and Jeoffrey sat at Lester's feet as he poured kibble into a bowl and talked to them. "I'll do it," I said, patting him on the shoulder. "You listen for the pizza man."

There was a pounding at the door. "Let me pay," Lester said. "My treat."

I knelt down and for the first time got a really good look at striped Jeoffrey. If I didn't know better, I wouldn't have suspected he was blind. His beautiful gold eyes simply had a faraway, contemplative look in them, and he carried his head cocked to one side as though he were listening for something. Well, maybe he was.

"Jeoffrey," I said, stroking him with my mitten. " 'For I will consider my cat, Jeoffrey,' " I told him, quoting from mad Christopher Smart's wonderful 300-year-old poem:

> For there is nothing sweeter than his peace
> when at rest;
> For there is nothing brisker than his life when
> in motion;
> For every house is incompleat without him,
> And a blessing is lacking in the spirit.

He turned his head toward me.

"Hi, guy," I said. "Glad to have you here."

He purred, and I looked over at Repo. "Show him the ropes," I said. "You know — litter pan, rag box, catnip plants, scratching post. The back stairs to Malcolm and Yvonne's. The best sunning spots."

"Mraff," Repo agreed.

239

Lester came back, carrying the pizza. "I met some kids coming up your walk," he said. "They're trick or treating. I put that basket of apples I picked out on the front porch with a sign for them to help themselves."

"Help themselves?" I asked.

"Yeah. It's Hallowe'en."

"Hallowe'en?" I straightened up, surprised. How could it be? Where had the days gone? And to think I almost missed it, as I had year after year. Well, I wouldn't miss it this time. I would finally keep my promise. "Hallowe'en," I repeated. "Of course it is. Hey, there's something I have to do."

"You do?" he asked warily. "Tonight?"

"Uh huh. Say, did you get those leaves bagged?"

"Er, no," he said. "I'll do that tomorrow."

"You won't need to," I said. "Take a look in that drawer, will you. The one beside the stove. There should be some matches toward the back."

While he was rummaging through the drawer, I darted into the bedroom and eased a heavy wool pullover on over my sweatshirt. I met him back in the kitchen.

"Got 'em," he said, a quizzical expression on his face. "Do you want me to build a fire?"

"Sort of," I said. "But we'll do it in the back yard. We're going to light a *Samhnagen*," I told him. "Bet you've never done that before."

He looked at me apprehensively. "Caitlin, are you sure you feel okay?"

"Yeah," I said. "I feel okay. And in a few minutes, I'm going to feel better than okay. I'm going to feel *good*. Come on, kiddo."

* * * * *

Outside, under the stars, we shivered a little in the late night chill. "You're sure this will be all right?" he asked nervously, eyeing the pile of leaves.

"Well, the Oak Bay Fire Department might come, but we'll just tell them we're burning garden debris." I winked at him. "No problem."

He held the matches uncertainly in one hand. "Is this, you know, some kind of ritual?" he asked. "A ceremony?"

"That's it exactly," I told him. "A ceremony. A throwback to my Celtic ancestors. Oh, by the way, did you leave the back door open like I asked you to?"

He nodded.

"Okay. Light the fire."

He struck a match, and bending, touched it to the pile of dry leaves. They caught instantly, and he stepped back. "Now what?" he asked.

"Now we wait," I told him.

"What for?" he whispered.

"We'll know when it happens," I whispered back.

The fire grew until the entire pile of leaves was burning, sending sparks shooting into the night sky. It turned Lester's face a ruddy orange, and for one glorious moment lit up the entire back yard, sending a dazzle of light high into the night sky. I raised my face to the moon, trying to follow the path of the sparks. How high did they rise, I wondered. Would it be high enough? Could the souls of the dead really see anything? Meadhbh, Mary, Judith, the dead animals, all the innocents — could they see my *Samnhagen?* And Meadhbh: would she come?

The fire began to burn down, smoking a little, and a brisk wind from the sea came scudding across the yard, twisting smoke and sparks together into fantastic shapes. One last flurry of light leaped high into the night air, an explosion of reddish gold motes like a school of copper minnows darting through dark seas, and from the house came a resounding *whamp*.

I thought Lester would jump out of his Air Jordans. "The, um," he cleared his throat, his voice dropping an octave, "the wind. Just the wind." He laughed nervously, hands jammed in his pockets, muttering to himself. "I thought for a minute someone went inside. But it was just the wind."

I looked over at the closed back door of my house and smiled. The wind? I knew better.

"Are you disappointed?" he asked softly.

"What?"

"Are you disappointed? Because, you know, nothing happened."

"No," I said, smiling, "I'm not disappointed."

"Good," he said, teeth chattering a little.

"C'mon," I told him. "Let's go in. It's cold out here, and I have a visitor to take care of."

He looked at me in wary puzzlement for a moment, then nodded quickly. "Oh yeah, your new cat."

I patted his shoulder, not wanting to confound him with too much truth all at once. "Right." I said. "Him, too."

Author's Note

Although this book is a work of fiction, the testing of cosmetics on animals is a fact. People wishing to purchase "cruelty-free" shampoo, soap, etc. are encouraged to write to the address below for a list of companies that do not test on animals, and for educational material.

People for the Ethical Treatment of Animals
P.O. Box 42516
Washington, DC 20015

BODY GUARD by Claire McNab. 224 pp. A Carol Ashton Mystery. 6th in a series. ISBN 1-56280-073-6 $9.95

CACTUS LOVE by Lee Lynch. 192 pp. Stories by the beloved storyteller. ISBN 1-56280-071-X 9.95

SECOND GUESS by Rose Beecham. 216 pp. An Amanda Valentine Mystery. 2nd in a series. ISBN 1-56280-069-8 9.95

THE SURE THING by Melissa Hartman. 208 pp. L.A. earthquake romance. ISBN 1-56280-078-7 9.95

A RAGE OF MAIDENS by Lauren Wright Douglas. 240 pp. A Caitlin Reece Mystery. 6th in a series. ISBN 1-56280-068-X 9.95

TRIPLE EXPOSURE by Jackie Calhoun. 224 pp. Romantic drama involving many characters. ISBN 1-56280-067-1 9.95

UP, UP AND AWAY by Catherine Ennis. 192 pp. Delightful romance. ISBN 1-56280-065-5 9.95

PERSONAL ADS by Robbi Sommers. 176 pp. Sizzling short stories. ISBN 1-56280-059-0 9.95

FLASHPOINT by Katherine V. Forrest. 256 pp. Lesbian blockbuster! ISBN 1-56280-043-4 22.95

CROSSWORDS by Penny Sumner. 256 pp. 2nd Victoria Cross Mystery. ISBN 1-56280-064-7 9.95

SWEET CHERRY WINE by Carol Schmidt. 224 pp. A novel of suspense. ISBN 1-56280-063-9 9.95

CERTAIN SMILES by Dorothy Tell. 160 pp. Erotic short stories. ISBN 1-56280-066-3 9.95

EDITED OUT by Lisa Haddock. 224 pp. 1st Carmen Ramirez Mystery. ISBN 1-56280-077-9 9.95

WEDNESDAY NIGHTS by Camarin Grae. 288 pp. Sexy adventure. ISBN 1-56280-060-4 10.95

SMOKEY O by Celia Cohen. 176 pp. Relationships on the playing field. ISBN 1-56280-057-4 9.95

KATHLEEN O'DONALD by Penny Hayes. 256 pp. Rose and Kathleen find each other and employment in 1909 NYC.
ISBN 1-56280-070-1   9.95

STAYING HOME by Elisabeth Nonas. 256 pp. Molly and Alix want a baby . . . or do they?   ISBN 1-56280-076-0   10.95

TRUE LOVE by Jennifer Fulton. 240 pp. Six lesbians searching for love in all the "right" places.   ISBN 1-56280-035-3   9.95

GARDENIAS WHERE THERE ARE NONE by Molleen Zanger. 176 pp. Why is Melanie inextricably drawn to the old house?
ISBN 1-56280-056-6   9.95

MICHAELA by Sarah Aldridge. 256 pp. A "Sarah Aldridge" romance.   ISBN 1-56280-055-8   10.95

KEEPING SECRETS by Penny Mickelbury. 208 pp. A Gianna Maglione Mystery. First in a series.   ISBN 1-56280-052-3   9.95

THE ROMANTIC NAIAD edited by Katherine V. Forrest & Barbara Grier. 336 pp. Love stories by Naiad Press authors.
ISBN 1-56280-054-X   14.95

UNDER MY SKIN by Jaye Maiman. 336 pp. A Robin Miller mystery. 3rd in a series.   ISBN 1-56280-049-3.   10.95

STAY TOONED by Rhonda Dicksion. 144 pp. Cartoons — 1st collection since Lesbian Survival Manual.   ISBN 1-56280-045-0   9.95

CAR POOL by Karin Kallmaker. 272pp. Lesbians on wheels and then some!   ISBN 1-56280-048-5   9.95

NOT TELLING MOTHER: STORIES FROM A LIFE by Diane Salvatore. 176 pp. Her 3rd novel.   ISBN 1-56280-044-2   9.95

GOBLIN MARKET by Lauren Wright Douglas. 240pp. A Caitlin Reece Mystery. 5th in a series.   ISBN 1-56280-047-7   9.95

LONG GOODBYES by Nikki Baker. 256 pp. A Virginia Kelly mystery. 3rd in a series.   ISBN 1-56280-042-6   9.95

FRIENDS AND LOVERS by Jackie Calhoun. 224 pp. Mid-western Lesbian lives and loves.   ISBN 1-56280-041-8   9.95

THE CAT CAME BACK by Hilary Mullins. 208 pp. Highly praised Lesbian novel.   ISBN 1-56280-040-X   9.95

BEHIND CLOSED DOORS by Robbi Sommers. 192 pp. Hot, erotic short stories.   ISBN 1-56280-039-6   9.95

CLAIRE OF THE MOON by Nicole Conn. 192 pp. See the movie — read the book!   ISBN 1-56280-038-8   10.95

SILENT HEART by Claire McNab. 192 pp. Exotic Lesbian romance.   ISBN 1-56280-036-1   9.95

HAPPY ENDINGS by Kate Brandt. 272 pp. Intimate conversations with Lesbian authors.   ISBN 1-56280-050-7   10.95

THE SPY IN QUESTION by Amanda Kyle Williams. 256 pp. 4th
Madison McGuire.   ISBN 1-56280-037-X   9.95

SAVING GRACE by Jennifer Fulton. 240 pp. Adventure and
romantic entanglement.   ISBN 1-56280-051-5   9.95

THE YEAR SEVEN by Molleen Zanger. 208 pp. Women surviving
in a new world.   ISBN 1-56280-034-5   9.95

CURIOUS WINE by Katherine V. Forrest. 176 pp. Tenth
Anniversary Edition. The most popular contemporary Lesbian
love story.   ISBN 1-56280-053-1   10.95

CHAUTAUQUA by Catherine Ennis. 192 pp. Exciting, romantic
adventure.   ISBN 1-56280-032-9   9.95

A PROPER BURIAL by Pat Welch. 192 pp. A Helen Black
mystery. 3rd in a series.   ISBN 1-56280-033-7   9.95

SILVERLAKE HEAT: A Novel of Suspense by Carol Schmidt.
240 pp. Rhonda is as hot as Laney's dreams.   ISBN 1-56280-031-0   9.95

LOVE, ZENA BETH by Diane Salvatore. 224 pp. The most talked
about lesbian novel of the nineties!   ISBN 1-56280-030-2   9.95

A DOORYARD FULL OF FLOWERS by Isabel Miller. 160 pp.
Stories incl. 2 sequels to *Patience and Sarah.*   ISBN 1-56280-029-9   9.95

MURDER BY TRADITION by Katherine V. Forrest. 288 pp. A
Kate Delafield Mystery. 4th in a series. ISBN 1-56280-002-7   9.95

THE EROTIC NAIAD edited by Katherine V. Forrest & Barbara Grier.
224 pp. Love stories by Naiad Press authors.   ISBN 1-56280-026-4   12.95

DEAD CERTAIN by Claire McNab. 224 pp. A Carol Ashton
mystery. 5th in a series.   ISBN 1-56280-027-2   9.95

CRAZY FOR LOVING by Jaye Maiman. 320 pp. A Robin Miller
mystery. 2nd in a series.   ISBN 1-56280-025-6   9.95

STONEHURST by Barbara Johnson. 176 pp. Passionate regency
romance.   ISBN 1-56280-024-8   9.95

INTRODUCING AMANDA VALENTINE by Rose Beecham.
256 pp. An Amanda Valentine Mystery. First in a series.
                                          ISBN 1-56280-021-3   9.95

UNCERTAIN COMPANIONS by Robbi Sommers. 204 pp.
Steamy, erotic novel.   ISBN 1-56280-017-5   9.95

A TIGER'S HEART by Lauren W. Douglas. 240 pp. A Caitlin
Reece mystery. 4th in a series.   ISBN 1-56280-018-3   9.95

PAPERBACK ROMANCE by Karin Kallmaker. 256 pp. A
delicious romance.   ISBN 1-56280-019-1   9.95

MORTON RIVER VALLEY by Lee Lynch. 304 pp. Lee Lynch at
her best!   ISBN 1-56280-016-7   9.95

THE LAVENDER HOUSE MURDER by Nikki Baker. 224 pp. A
Virginia Kelly Mystery. 2nd in a series. ISBN 1-56280-012-4   9.95

PASSION BAY by Jennifer Fulton. 224 pp. Passionate romance, virgin beaches, tropical skies. ISBN 1-56280-028-0   9.95

STICKS AND STONES by Jackie Calhoun. 208 pp. Contemporary lesbian lives and loves. ISBN 1-56280-020-5   9.95

DELIA IRONFOOT by Jeane Harris. 192 pp. Adventure for Delia and Beth in the Utah mountains. ISBN 1-56280-014-0   9.95

UNDER THE SOUTHERN CROSS by Claire McNab. 192 pp. Romantic nights Down Under. ISBN 1-56280-011-6   9.95

RIVERFINGER WOMEN by Elana Nachman/Dykewomon. 208 pp. Classic Lesbian/feminist novel. ISBN 1-56280-013-2   8.95

GRASSY FLATS by Penny Hayes. 256 pp. Lesbian romance in the '30s. ISBN 1-56280-010-8   9.95

A SINGULAR SPY by Amanda K. Williams. 192 pp. 3rd Madison McGuire. ISBN 1-56280-008-6   8.95

THE END OF APRIL by Penny Sumner. 240 pp. A Victoria Cross Mystery. First in a series. ISBN 1-56280-007-8   8.95

A FLIGHT OF ANGELS by Sarah Aldridge. 240 pp. Romance set at the National Gallery of Art ISBN 1-56280-001-9   9.95

HOUSTON TOWN by Deborah Powell. 208 pp. A Hollis Carpenter mystery. Second in a series. ISBN 1-56280-006-X   8.95

KISS AND TELL by Robbi Sommers. 192 pp. Scorching stories by the author of *Pleasures*. ISBN 1-56280-005-1   9.95

STILL WATERS by Pat Welch. 208 pp. A Helen Black mystery. 2nd in a series. ISBN 0-941483-97-5   9.95

TO LOVE AGAIN by Evelyn Kennedy. 208 pp. Wildly romantic love story. ISBN 0-941483-85-1   9.95

IN THE GAME by Nikki Baker. 192 pp. A Virginia Kelly mystery. First in a series. ISBN 1-56280-004-3   9.95

AVALON by Mary Jane Jones. 256 pp. A Lesbian Arthurian romance. ISBN 0-941483-96-7   9.95

STRANDED by Camarin Grae. 320 pp. Entertaining, riveting adventure. ISBN 0-941483-99-1   9.95

THE DAUGHTERS OF ARTEMIS by Lauren Wright Douglas. 240 pp. A Caitlin Reece mystery. 3rd in a series. ISBN 0-941483-95-9   9.95

CLEARWATER by Catherine Ennis. 176 pp. Romantic secrets of a small Louisiana town. ISBN 0-941483-65-7   8.95

THE HALLELUJAH MURDERS by Dorothy Tell. 176 pp. A Poppy Dillworth mystery. 2nd in a series. ISBN 0-941483-88-6   8.95

SECOND CHANCE by Jackie Calhoun. 256 pp. Contemporary Lesbian lives and loves. ISBN 0-941483-93-2   9.95

BENEDICTION by Diane Salvatore. 272 pp. Striking,
contemporary romantic novel.   ISBN 0-941483-90-8   9.95

BLACK IRIS by Jeane Harris. 192 pp. Caroline's hidden past . . .
                                                ISBN 0-941483-68-1   8.95

TOUCHWOOD by Karin Kallmaker. 240 pp. Loving, May/
December romance.   ISBN 0-941483-76-2   9.95

COP OUT by Claire McNab. 208 pp. A Carol Ashton mystery.
4th in a series.   ISBN 0-941483-84-3   9.95

THE BEVERLY MALIBU by Katherine V. Forrest. 288 pp. A
Kate Delafield Mystery. 3rd in a series.   ISBN 0-941483-48-7   9.95

THAT OLD STUDEBAKER by Lee Lynch. 272 pp. Andy's affair
with Regina and her attachment to her beloved car.
                                                ISBN 0-941483-82-7   9.95

PASSION'S LEGACY by Lori Paige. 224 pp. Sarah is swept into
the arms of Augusta Pym in this delightful historical romance.
                                                ISBN 0-941483-81-9   8.95

THE PROVIDENCE FILE by Amanda Kyle Williams. 256 pp.
Second Madison McGuire   ISBN 0-941483-92-4   8.95

I LEFT MY HEART by Jaye Maiman. 320 pp. A Robin Miller
Mystery. First in a series.   ISBN 0-941483-72-X   9.95

THE PRICE OF SALT by Patricia Highsmith (writing as Claire
Morgan). 288 pp. Classic lesbian novel, first issued in 1952 . . .
acknowledged by its author under her own, very famous, name.
                                                ISBN 1-56280-003-5   9.95

SIDE BY SIDE by Isabel Miller. 256 pp. From beloved author of
Patience and Sarah.   ISBN 0-941483-77-0   9.95

STAYING POWER: LONG TERM LESBIAN COUPLES
by Susan E. Johnson. 352 pp. Joys of coupledom.
                                                ISBN 0-941-483-75-4   12.95

SLICK by Camarin Grae. 304 pp. Exotic, erotic adventure.
                                                ISBN 0-941483-74-6   9.95

NINTH LIFE by Lauren Wright Douglas. 256 pp. A Caitlin
Reece mystery. 2nd in a series.   ISBN 0-941483-50-9   8.95

PLAYERS by Robbi Sommers. 192 pp. Sizzling, erotic novel.
                                                ISBN 0-941483-73-8   9.95

MURDER AT RED ROOK RANCH by Dorothy Tell. 224 pp.
A Poppy Dillworth mystery. 1st in a series.   ISBN 0-941483-80-0   8.95

LESBIAN SURVIVAL MANUAL by Rhonda Dicksion.
112 pp. Cartoons!   ISBN 0-941483-71-1   8.95

A ROOM FULL OF WOMEN by Elisabeth Nonas. 256 pp.
Contemporary Lesbian lives.   ISBN 0-941483-69-X   9.95

THEME FOR DIVERSE INSTRUMENTS by Jane Rule. 208
pp. Powerful romantic lesbian stories. ISBN 0-941483-63-0   8.95

LESBIAN QUERIES by Hertz & Ertman. 112 pp. The questions
you were too embarrassed to ask. ISBN 0-941483-67-3   8.95

CLUB 12 by Amanda Kyle Williams. 288 pp. Espionage thriller
featuring a lesbian agent! ISBN 0-941483-64-9   8.95

DEATH DOWN UNDER by Claire McNab. 240 pp. A Carol
Ashton mystery. 3rd in a series. ISBN 0-941483-39-8   9.95

MONTANA FEATHERS by Penny Hayes. 256 pp. Vivian and
Elizabeth find love in frontier Montana. ISBN 0-941483-61-4   8.95

LIFESTYLES by Jackie Calhoun. 224 pp. Contemporary Lesbian
lives and loves. ISBN 0-941483-57-6   9.95

WILDERNESS TREK by Dorothy Tell. 192 pp. Six women on
vacation learning "new" skills. ISBN 0-941483-60-6   8.95

MURDER BY THE BOOK by Pat Welch. 256 pp. A Helen
Black Mystery. First in a series. ISBN 0-941483-59-2   9.95

THERE'S SOMETHING I'VE BEEN MEANING TO TELL
YOU Ed. by Loralee MacPike. 288 pp. Gay men and lesbians
coming out to their children. ISBN 0-941483-44-4   9.95

LIFTING BELLY by Gertrude Stein. Ed. by Rebecca Mark. 104
pp. Erotic poetry. ISBN 0-941483-51-7   8.95

AFTER THE FIRE by Jane Rule. 256 pp. Warm, human novel
by this incomparable author. ISBN 0-941483-45-2   8.95

THREE WOMEN by March Hastings. 232 pp. Golden oldie. A
triangle among wealthy sophisticates. ISBN 0-941483-43-6   8.95

PLEASURES by Robbi Sommers. 204 pp. Unprecedented
eroticism. ISBN 0-941483-49-5   8.95

EDGEWISE by Camarin Grae. 372 pp. Spellbinding
adventure. ISBN 0-941483-19-3   9.95

FATAL REUNION by Claire McNab. 224 pp. A Carol Ashton
mystery. 2nd in a series. ISBN 0-941483-40-1   8.95

KEEP TO ME STRANGER by Sarah Aldridge. 372 pp. Romance
set in a department store dynasty. ISBN 0-941483-38-X   9.95

IN EVERY PORT by Karin Kallmaker. 228 pp. Jessica's sexy,
adventuresome travels. ISBN 0-941483-37-7   9.95

OF LOVE AND GLORY by Evelyn Kennedy. 192 pp. Exciting
WWII romance. ISBN 0-941483-32-0   8.95

CLICKING STONES by Nancy Tyler Glenn. 288 pp. Love
transcending time. ISBN 0-941483-31-2   9.95

SURVIVING SISTERS by Gail Pass. 252 pp. Powerful love
story. ISBN 0-941483-16-9   8.95

SOUTH OF THE LINE by Catherine Ennis. 216 pp. Civil War
adventure.   ISBN 0-941483-29-0   8.95

WOMAN PLUS WOMAN by Dolores Klaich. 300 pp. Supurb
Lesbian overview.   ISBN 0-941483-28-2   9.95

THE FINER GRAIN by Denise Ohio. 216 pp. Brilliant young
college lesbian novel.   ISBN 0-941483-11-8   8.95

OCTOBER OBSESSION by Meredith More. Josie's rich, secret
Lesbian life.   ISBN 0-941483-18-5   8.95

BEFORE STONEWALL: THE MAKING OF A GAY AND
LESBIAN COMMUNITY by Andrea Weiss & Greta Schiller.
96 pp., 25 illus.   ISBN 0-941483-20-7   7.95

OSTEN'S BAY by Zenobia N. Vole. 204 pp. Sizzling adventure
romance set on Bonaire.   ISBN 0-941483-15-0   8.95

LESSONS IN MURDER by Claire McNab. 216 pp. A Carol
Ashton mystery. First in a series.   ISBN 0-941483-14-2   9.95

YELLOWTHROAT by Penny Hayes. 240 pp. Margarita, bandit,
kidnaps Julia.   ISBN 0-941483-10-X   8.95

SAPPHISTRY: THE BOOK OF LESBIAN SEXUALITY by
Pat Califia. 3d edition, revised. 208 pp.   ISBN 0-941483-24-X   10.95

CHERISHED LOVE by Evelyn Kennedy. 192 pp. Erotic
Lesbian love story.   ISBN 0-941483-08-8   9.95

THE SECRET IN THE BIRD by Camarin Grae. 312 pp. Striking,
psychological suspense novel.   ISBN 0-941483-05-3   8.95

TO THE LIGHTNING by Catherine Ennis. 208 pp. Romantic
Lesbian 'Robinson Crusoe' adventure.   ISBN 0-941483-06-1   8.95

DREAMS AND SWORDS by Katherine V. Forrest. 192 pp.
Romantic, erotic, imaginative stories. ISBN 0-941483-03-7   8.95

MEMORY BOARD by Jane Rule. 336 pp. Memorable novel
about an aging Lesbian couple.   ISBN 0-941483-02-9   9.95

THE ALWAYS ANONYMOUS BEAST by Lauren Wright
Douglas. 224 pp. A Caitlin Reece mystery. First in a series.
                                        ISBN 0-941483-04-5   8.95

These are just a few of the many Naiad Press titles — we are the oldest and
largest lesbian/feminist publishing company in the world. Please request a
complete catalog. We offer personal service; we encourage and welcome
ect mail orders from individuals who have limited access to bookstores
ng our publications.

The fence was fifteen yards way. Ten. Five. To hell with the last ten feet or so — I wanted to be airborne! I jumped — a leap Jackie Joyner Kersee would have been proud of — and swarmed up the mesh like an ape. I had one hand on the barbed wire when I felt something hit me just behind the knee. Something that bit.

"Aargh!" I yelled, kicking. One hand lost its grip on the wire as this heavy *something* pulled me down. I heard my jeans ripping, and suddenly I was free. Terror put my brain into neutral, freeing me from the necessity of thinking and the handicap of feeling pain. Instincts honed in the primordial ooze took over, sending me back up the fence like a gecko up a wall. "Oh shit, oh shit, oh shit," I gibbered as the Dobie jumped for me again, chomping down on my foot.

Fear gave me the strength of three ordinary women and I held onto the mesh this time. Then with one twisting lurch, I pulled my foot out of the shoe and left it to Fang. Boy, did I have leverage now! I bent my leg, stuck my shoeless toes into the mesh, threw my arms up and over the barbed wire, and pushed off. I went over the top like a diver off the low board, like a pole vaulter clearing sixteen feet, like a penitent seeking heaven. There was only one thing wrong. I had to come back down.

About the Author

Lauren Wright Douglas was born in Canada in 1947. She grew up in a military family and spent part of her childhood in Europe. She published her first short story at age twelve in the school newspaper,and since then has pursued a part-time career writing short stories, screenplays, magazine and newspaper articles, essays, poetry, and novels. To support this avocation, she has been a high school English teacher, a newspaper editor, a French translator, a college English teacher, a creative writing teacher for gifted high school students, a public relations person, and a grants writer. Lauren moved from Oak Bay, Victoria, British Columbia to the American Southwest some years ago where she now lives with her partner, six cats, and two rabbits.